Anika's Mountain

Anika's
Mountain

Karen Rispin

Tyndale House Publishers, Inc.
Wheaton, Illinois

Anika's Mountain

Karen Rispin

Tyndale House Publishers, Inc.
Wheaton, Illinois

Scripture quotations are from the *International Children's Bible, New Century Version,* copyright © 1986, 1988 by Word Publishing, Dallas, Texas 75039. Used by permission.

Library of Congress Cataloging-in-Publication Data

Rispin, Karen, date
  Anika's mountain / Karen Rispin.
     p.   cm. — (Anika Scott series : #3)
  Summary: Twelve-year-old Anika needs God's help while making the difficult climb to the top of Mount Kenya, and even more when she learns a family secret that she doesn't want to believe.
  ISBN 0-8423-1219-6 (softcover) :
  [1. Mountaineering—Fiction.   2. Family problems—Fiction.
3. Christian life—Fiction.] I. Title.   II. Series: Rispin, Karen,
1955-   Anika Scott : 3.
PZ7.R494An 1994   93-31345
[Fic]—dc20

Printed in the United States of America

00 99 98 97 96 95 94
7   6   5   4   3   2   1

To Phil

Chapter
One

∿∿∿∿∿∿∿∿∿

It seemed like a happy, lazy, sunny day. My sister and I had been home from boarding school for a week.

I woke up late. The corrugated metal roof was already making popping noises from the hot sun. Sandy's bed was empty. I could hear Mom and Barnabas, the African man who works for us, talking on the porch. I stretched and smiled. It was very good to be home.

A few minutes later I was hanging up sheets with Mom. The damp sheets blew cool against my cheeks as I reached up to peg them to the line.

"Ut uu ona uu uday," Mom said around the clothes-pins in her mouth.

"I don't know," I said, laughing. "I'll do whatever happens."

When the wash was done, I wandered across the station toward Lisa's house with the warm sun on my back. Lisa Barnes is my best friend.

Traci and Sandy followed me a few minutes later. Traci Stewart is ten, the same as Sandy. Her parents work at the Bible school too. She and her little brother, David, have been in Kenya ever since they were born. We ended up playing Monopoly with them.

"Did you hear that?" Traci hissed suddenly. She dropped her Monopoly money, jerked her chair forward, and said, "Listen!"

Without paying attention, I'd been hearing Lisa's dad talking to someone on their porch. He was bellowing, really, but that's normal for him.

"It's just my dad," Lisa said.

"It's Uncle Joey. So what?" Sandy said at the same time.

"Listen to what he's saying!" Traci insisted.

". . . we hustle, we could be heading up the mountain tomorrow." Uncle Joey's voice came in loud and clear even though he was out on the porch.

"Mountain?" Lisa muttered. "What mountain?"

I caught my breath. Could he be talking about climbing Mount Kenya, or maybe even Mount Kilimanjaro? Those were the two biggest mountains in my world.

". . . two-day hike," Uncle Joey was saying. "Mark said he'd lend us gear. If we can't have winter, we can at least find the kids some snow on the top of Mount Kenya. Wouldn't want them to forget what it is." His laugh boomed through the wall.

Mount Kenya, I thought, *and he's taking kids!* A wave of prickly electricity washed through me. Maybe

. . . maybe he'd let me come. I knew people who had climbed. Some of the older kids at school had. It's hard to make it to the top. People notice the ones who make it. No kids in my grade had even tried.

"Lisa," I said, reaching for her arm. "If you guys go, I want to come too. You've got to get your dad to let me come with you. Please?"

"Me too," said Sandy, shoving her chair back.

Traci jumped up, bumping the table. Houses and hotels flew in all directions. "It's not fair if you guys get to go and I don't! I'm coming too. Can I, Lisa? Can I?"

Lisa stared at us with her mouth open. She hadn't been in Kenya very long. *Still,* I thought, *she should know by now how important the mountain is.*

I sighed and said, "Mount Kenya, you know, Mount Kenya! Right? The one you can see from a hundred miles away. The biggest mountain in Kenya, the one they named the country—"

"Stop it!" she said. "I know about the mountain, but why do you guys want—"

"Shhhh! Listen!" Traci said.

"You think I'll bite off more than I can chew, do you?" Uncle Joey said, and he laughed again. "I don't know about that. I've heard that kids as young as nine years old have made it up to Lenana Peak. I'm a pretty tough old hombre, and my kids aren't wimps either."

Lisa rolled her eyes and whispered, "Da-ad!" She hates it when her dad does the hearty-American act.

"Who's he talking to?" Sandy asked.

I shrugged. Whoever it was didn't talk as loud as Uncle Joey, but that didn't narrow it down much.

Traci suddenly headed for the door. "I'm going to ask my mom and dad. If they say OK, Lisa's dad can't say no."

"Me too. Come on, Anika!" Sandy said and bolted out the door.

I jittered nervously on one foot. I didn't think Traci was right, but it wouldn't hurt to ask Mom and Daddy. I could hardly believe that Uncle Joey wanted his kids to climb. Maybe some nine-year-old did make it up once. He must have either been practically Superboy or his father carried him. I'm twelve, and if there was any chance at all, I didn't intend to miss it. If I could just get Lisa to ask her dad to bring me . . .

"Look, Lisa," I said. "We're friends, right?"

"No way, a geek like you?" she said, but she grinned.

"Come on, you've got to listen," I begged. "I've wanted to climb Mount Kenya forever, and now you'll get to go. Please, you've got to get your parents to let me come with you. Ask for me, please?"

"OK, OK! I'll ask already. You guys are nuts," she said and then grinned. "Besides, I want you to come anyway if I have to climb up that mountain."

"Don't you *want* to?" I asked in a voice that squeaked with surprise.

She shook her head.

"Why not?" I asked. Then without giving her time to answer, I blurted, "I've got to go before Sandy wrecks it with Mom and Daddy. You're the greatest, Lisa!"

My stomach was in a tight knot. "Please, God, let it work. Let me get to climb with Lisa," I prayed under my breath as I trotted up the hill. The peaceful mood of the day was completely shattered.

All I could think about was Mount Kenya. I wanted to climb so much it ached. Mountains had always seemed magic to me. Among all the mountains I knew, Mount Kenya was best. It wasn't flat on top like Kilimanjaro, or just part of a long string of peaks like the Rocky Mountains I'd seen in Canada. It was a perfect mountain, all alone with three high, jagged peaks.

I whispered their names, "Nelion, Mbatian, and Lenana." The names of three Masai chiefs. Nelion and Mbatian were the highest. One could only climb there with ropes and special gear. Lenana was the one normal people climbed.

"Lenana," I whispered again. I would get there if I could, if I possibly could. Not watching where I was going, I ran smack into Traci's father.

"Take it easy," Uncle Paul said, catching me.

"Daddy, tell her! Tell her!" Traci said, jumping up and down holding on to her dad's arm. "We're going! I get to go up Mount Kenya!"

He just smiled in his big red beard.

"Well, we are!" Traci said, tossing her head to flip her hair off her face. Then she looked at her dad and added, "Maybe."

"What? When? I mean . . ." I stuttered, trying to decide what to ask first. Uncle Paul's blue eyes twinkled like he was laughing at me. I blurted, "Never mind!" and ran for home.

It wasn't any use waiting for Uncle Paul to explain. He only talks when he absolutely has to. My thongs slapped hard on the concrete floor of our porch as I skidded to a halt. I yanked the screen open and let it slam behind me. I didn't know it yet, but the chance to climb a mountain was a small thing compared to what was about to touch my life that day.

"Mom!" I yelled. All I could hear was my own breath, panting from running. Sandy must have gone down to Daddy's office instead. Still, Mom should be here.

"Mom!" I yelled again, hurrying down the hall to her office. She was there, sitting at her desk with a letter in her hand. She quickly slid the letter under a book and turned her head away from me.

"Mom," I blurted, "you've got to let me go. Barneses

are—" I stopped, feeling very odd. Mom still hadn't looked at me and her shoulders were heaving. I could hear her crying. Mom never cries. Something was horribly wrong.

"Mom?" My voice came out small and high.

She took a deep breath and, without turning, said, "Anika, just leave me be for now. Go out and shut the door."

"But . . . but . . . ," I stammered. My thoughts felt the way a line of pinching ants looks when you blow on them. First they're all running along in a line. You blow, and they scatter, running in wild circles.

"Please," Mom said, crying again, "just go."

I backed out, shut the door, and stood staring at it with my heart hammering in my ears. It had to be that letter she'd hidden.

The house didn't feel safe anymore. I walked slowly out and sat on the porch rail. Sunshine lay across my shoulders like a warm, comforting hand.

My thoughts still ran around like excited ants. What was wrong? Maybe somebody had died, but she'd tell me that, wouldn't she? What if Daddy was sick again, I wondered, and my stomach tightened into a hard knot. What if the letter was a doctor's report about Daddy saying he was going to die? He'd been so sick before. But he had been getting better and better. . . .

I looked at his office and let out my breath in relief. Daddy was OK. I could see him walking across to the Barneses' with Sandy.

I looked away, then my head snapped back to stare. Walking across to the Barneses' with Sandy! He was going to talk about climbing the mountain. He was. He had to be.

I was on my feet with a lunge and off to Barneses' house.

Five other kids were on the low cinder block wall around Barneses' porch. Besides Lisa, Traci Stewart, and Sandy, there was Lisa's little brother, Alex, and David Stewart. The two boys were play fighting, both trying to sit in the same spot.

"They won't let us in," Traci said, flipping her red hair out of her eyes.

"Who?" I demanded, skidding to a halt.

"Daddy, Uncle Joey, and Uncle Paul. They're deciding if we can go," Sandy said, jumping to her feet. "*I* got Daddy to come. *I* got Daddy to come," she added in a singsong voice, hopping on one foot. She stopped and suddenly demanded, "Where did you go, anyway?"

What Sandy said made me suddenly remember Mom crying. It gave me a sick feeling. To shut it out I snapped at Sandy, "You're too little to climb anyway!" I felt bad the second the words were out of my mouth.

"I am not!" she yelled. "I heard Uncle Joey say kids as young as nine have gone!"

"Nine?" David Stewart asked, popping up suddenly from where Alex had shoved him off the porch rail into the flower garden. "Hey, all right Alex!" He shoved Alex, and Alex slithered onto the porch floor and sat up staring at us with his mouse brown hair sticking out in all directions.

"That means we can go," David said, hopping back onto the wall. "Dad said he was going, right, Traci?"

Shoving the misery out of my mind, I focused on Traci. If they got to go, there was a good chance we would. Traci squirmed and looked at her feet without answering.

"You said!" David said, jumping to his feet and sticking his hands on his hips.

Traci glared at him and said, "Dad said *he* might go if it was OK or whatever."

"What about us?" David demanded again.

"He didn't say," she said. She looked at Lisa out of the corner of her eye and added, "He only laughed when I said I was tougher than Lisa anyway. He said none of us had a foggy notion what we were getting into, and that people die up there."

"They die?" said Lisa in a squeak. "You guys are nuts. I'll stay at the bottom and sing at your funeral, OK?"

I clenched my teeth. Why did Traci have to go talk about dying?

"They don't die," I said, sitting down by Lisa and glaring at Traci. "What about the big kids at school that have climbed?"

"Dad said!" Traci insisted.

My stomach felt hollow thinking about people dying. Uncle Paul doesn't lie. I swallowed hard. If other people could climb it, so could I. I could! I stuck my chin up and said, "Well, those people probably just did something stupid. We'll be careful, right, Lisa?"

Lisa didn't have time to answer, because David burst in. "If a girl can climb, we can too," he said, poking Alex.

Just then Daddy walked out of the house.

"Are we going?" I asked, jumping to my feet. At the same time Sandy said, "People don't die, do they?"

Daddy gave her a funny look and said, "Everyone dies eventually, Sandy, and we *are* going—home for supper, that is."

Both of us said, "Daddeeee!"

He wouldn't say anything else on the walk up to the house.

At the house door I stopped, so that Sandy and Daddy went in ahead of me. Hovering behind the door, I heard Mom talking to Sandy and Daddy in a normal voice. I edged around the door. The house seemed warm and safe, and I could smell meat loaf cooking for supper. Sandy and Daddy started telling Mom about climbing Mount Kenya.

While we ate supper, the others talked and I watched Mom. She seemed to be acting normal. I *had* seen her crying, hadn't I? I glanced at her again. Maybe her eyes were a little red. I couldn't be sure.

". . . and we heard Uncle Joey say he's taking Lisa and Alex," Sandy was saying.

"Where did Uncle Joey come up with this?" Mom asked, cutting into her baked potato. Then she stopped and looked hard at Daddy. "Kevin, are you sure you ought to do this, anyway? You've hardly finished recuperating."

"Oh, I'm not thinking about climbing," Daddy said.

My heart dropped right to my feet, but then he went on. "What I want to do is fish."

"Fish?!" I blurted without thinking. "Fish on a mountain?"

Daddy grinned at me. "They're special rock fish that live only on snow-covered volcanic peaks."

"Daddeeee!" I said. "This is serious."

"OK, OK. The stream that runs by Forest Lodge has been stocked with rainbow trout. I haven't had a trout on a fly line for years. So you guys go climb the mountain. While you're struggling up icy glaciers in thin summer clothes, I'll be having fun."

11

"You still haven't told me where Joey came up with this wild scheme," Mom reminded him.

"Mark Jeremias," Daddy said. "Joey met him in Nairobi. Apparently Mark had planned to take a group up that was coming in from England, but they had to cancel. I didn't hear why. Anyway, he offered Joey the bookings at the lodge and the overnight hut on the mountain. The people in the group couldn't get their money back at this late date in any case. They asked him to find someone who could use their bookings."

"How much would it cost?" Mom asked.

I held my breath for Daddy's answer. Money can wreck so many things.

"Apparently the men in the group told Mark to give them away if he could find someone to take them."

"All right!" I interrupted. "God is giving us a present, so we have to go."

"Anika," Mom said, "don't leap to conclusions."

"What's with you, Hazel?" Daddy asked. "I thought you'd be excited about this. You've talked about wanting to climb Mount Kenya. Joey wants us and the Stewarts to come over to his place after supper to talk about it."

"Kids too?" I asked.

"Absolutely not," he said. Sandy and I groaned.

"Kevin, there is something you and I have to talk

about before we can make any plans," Mom said in a tight voice.

"Well?" Daddy asked.

"Later," Mom said, glancing at Sandy and me.

I looked hard at Mom, wanting to ask if it was that letter that made her cry.

"Does that mean that you're not going to the meeting?" Sandy demanded suddenly. "You have to! If you don't it will wreck everything!"

I kicked her under the table to make her back off. She kicked me back hard and glared at me.

Daddy looked thoughtfully at Mom and said, "We'll go to find out what's happening. You and I can talk later."

Mom frowned, but said, "If that's what you want."

"OK!" Sandy yelled.

"You two will have to put yourselves to bed," Mom said.

Sandy nodded eagerly. "We will! We'll go to bed early too, right, Anika? In case we get to go tomorrow."

"It won't be tomorrow in any case," Daddy said. "The reservations are for the day after tomorrow."

I wasn't sure things were OK at all. It wasn't fair. Why did whatever it was have to happen now, just when I might have a chance at Mount Kenya with Lisa?

Chapter Two

"I just know we're going to go!" Sandy said as soon as they were out the door. She spun around the room singing, "Going on a mountain climb! I'm not afraid!"

Sandy stopped spinning just long enough to grab a couple of plates and dance toward the kitchen with them. I watched her with my stomach tight with worry.

She didn't stay quiet for long. "Hey, do you think we'll have porters, or carry our own stuff?"

I shrugged and shoved the plug into the sink.

"What's wrong with you?" Sandy asked, stopping and staring at me.

Trying to push away worry about the letter that made Mom cry, I said, "We don't even have any warm clothes, and besides, they'll probably say we're too young to climb."

That made me feel worse. It didn't bother Sandy, though.

"Hey, I know," she said. "We should figure out warm clothes. Like maybe we could put grass or something inside our shirts, then they can't make us not climb."

"Yuck!" I said. "That would itch." It made me squirm just thinking about it. Sandy was right, though. We had to figure out how to get warm clothes, or they wouldn't let us climb. In my head, in some silly way everything seemed tied to the need for warm clothes. I frowned, thinking hard.

"Hey! I know!" I blurted, dropping the dishcloth. "We can put on layers of clothes. Come on!" I grabbed Sandy's hand. "It will work! I know it."

A few minutes later we had clothes all over our bedroom trying to figure out which things would go on top of each other best.

I stuffed on two T-shirts and two sweatshirts, then pulled on an old red sweater over that. Sandy had put on so many pants that she looked like a gingerbread man.

She giggled and waddled around the room. My arms stuck stiffly out. I nearly lost my balance trying to bend them enough to get another pair of pants on and fell onto my bed giggling.

"I can just see us climbing the mountain," Sandy said, waddling like a marching teddy bear. "At least it won't hurt if we fall over a cliff."

"I get it! The whole trouble is that the outside layer is

too tight. So we just need to put on bigger clothes on the outside. Look, you put on my stuff for the top two layers, and I'll get some of Mom's."

"You aren't allowed!" Sandy called as I ran downstairs to Mom and Daddy's room.

"She won't mind," I said and added under my breath, "I hope."

My idea of putting bigger clothes on top worked. Well, at least we could move freely if we didn't trip over the dragging pant legs. We nearly killed ourselves laughing. My hair stuck to my forehead with sweat from laughing inside so many hot clothes. We kept trying on different things to see what would work best, and just because it was fun. After a bit both of us had about nine layers on, and the top one was Dad's clothes. We were standing in front of the mirror in Mom and Dad's room giggling when we heard the front door open and Daddy talking.

We stared wildly at each other and started frantically yanking off clothes. The dishes weren't done. There were clothes all over both bedrooms, and we weren't in bed. It's harder to get clothes off in a hurry than you'd think. Especially when you have on nine or ten layers like we did. Halfway out of Daddy's big gray sweater I stopped and stood there. We didn't have a hope.

Sandy gave me a panicked look, fell to her knees, and crawled under Mom and Daddy's bed.

"What on earth?" Dad was standing in the doorway with his mouth open.

"Kevin!" Mom screamed from upstairs. "Kevin, come here! The kids aren't in bed, and their room is all torn apart!"

"It's OK, Hazel," Daddy called. "They're here."

Mom pounded back downstairs and rushed into the room.

"Oh, thank goodness you're OK," she said, out of breath. "I thought for a second someone had broken in. Where's Sandy?" Then she did a double take and echoed Daddy, "What on earth?"

"I think you'll find your younger daughter under the bed," Daddy said in an odd, flat voice. I gave him a look. Was he trying not to laugh?

Mom bent over to look, and Sandy crawled out slowly. I'd been standing stock-still, with one arm still in Daddy's sweater. Now I sighed and pulled the sweater off over my head and started on the first layer of pants.

Mom stood up and looked around the room. "With ith thorst than the wids koom!" Mom is always getting her words tangled.

Daddy lost his struggle not to laugh and absolutely roared.

"It's not funny," Mom protested. "They were supposed to do the dishes and get into bed." But then she looked at us again, and suddenly she burst out laughing too.

Sandy and I grinned uneasily.

"Let me guess," Daddy said, still gasping with laughter. "Warm clothes for climbing, right?"

I nodded and blurted, "It would work. It would. If you put bigger clothes on top you can move OK. It will be warm enough, because I'm really hot."

"You look hot," Daddy said, looking me up and down and trying not to laugh again. "Now get out of those clothes, clean up this mess, and get into bed. Make sure you put our things back exactly the way you found them."

"I'll help," Mom said. "They won't get done until midnight otherwise."

While we were cleaning up, Sandy tried to get Mom to tell her what they'd decided at the meeting, but Mom wasn't talking. All she would say was that Daddy and she had to talk before they'd decide.

When we finally got to bed, I couldn't get to sleep. Mom's and Daddy's voices came up softly through the floor. I was sticky from getting so hot in all the clothes. A picture of Mom, hunched crying at her desk, flashed into my mind. I squirmed and flopped onto my back. Would she make us stay home?

Staring up at the ceiling, I saw a shadow pattern that looked almost like Mount Kenya. I focused on the top of the shadow mountain. Would I make it even if I did get to try? Suddenly the layers-of-clothes idea seemed silly.

I flopped onto my side. The top sheet stuck to my sweaty skin and got tangled. I jerked it loose so hard my whole bed came untucked. Sandy was snoring softly.

"Please God, let it be OK," I whispered. "I mean Mom, and getting to climb, and making it to the top, and everything."

One of the verses I'd read that morning came back into my head—something about being strong, him making us strong. I felt for my flashlight and pulled it and my Bible into bed with me. Then I ducked under the covers and switched the flashlight on. It took me a while to find the place.

It was in Ephesians. "I ask the Father in his great glory to give you the power to be strong in spirit. He will give you that strength through his Spirit," it said. "With God's power working in us, God can do much, much more than anything we can ask or think of."

"Please help me be strong, however you do it," I whispered. I got up to straighten my bed, then decided I'd better go down and go to the bathroom.

The bathroom is right across from Mom and Daddy's room. I froze with my hand on the doorknob. Mom was crying again.

"Hazel, Hazel, don't worry," Daddy was saying. "We've

had this all out years ago. The letter doesn't change anything between us. I love you."

Mom said something muffled that ended in ". . . about the kids?"

"They'll be fine. Kids are resilient. We've prayed for the child for fifteen years, ever since we got saved. Now this letter means that we may get to see him."

See who? I thought.

The bed creaked like someone was getting up, and I shot into the bathroom.

On the way out I paused again, but Mom and Daddy were talking more quietly. All I heard was Mom saying something like, ". . . not tell them just yet, maybe after the—"

Then Daddy interrupted with a very loud "Get to bed!" He'd heard me open the bathroom door.

I went up the stairs in a hurry. *Who aren't they going to tell just yet? Sandy and me?* I wondered as I climbed back into bed. Was that last word Mom was going to say *climb?* Did that mean we were going to get to go?

The questions chased themselves in circles in my head until they turned into odd dreams about secret agents attacking mountain climbers.

"Anika! Anika!" Sandy's yell brought me up out of sleep with a jerk. I blinked my eyes at the morning light and struggled to sit up.

"We get to go! We're going!" she said, jumping full length onto her own bed, then sitting up cross-legged.

"All of us?" I demanded.

She nodded with a big grin on her face.

"All right!" I yelled, leaping out of bed and forgetting everything but Mount Kenya.

That day was crazy. Daddy spent all day at the office trying to get everything ready for him to be gone, so packing was up to Mom and us. Mom still seemed kind of worried, but it was hard to tell in all the rush.

It turned out that Traci's mom and Lisa's weren't coming to the mountain with us. They weren't going to let Alex and David come either. They said the boys were too little. The noise Alex made about that was hardly to be believed.

"Listen, you two," Mom said to Sandy and me, "are you dure you want to shu this?"

"I'm absolutely dure," I managed to say between laughing. Sandy nodded too.

Mom didn't laugh. "Seriously, it's not going to be easy."

"We know," I said. "Lots of people don't make it to the top."

"We will, though," Sandy added solemnly.

Mom smiled at that, then looked at us both hard. "OK. If that's the way you want it, I'll try to find equipment for you."

After she left I went into her office, but I couldn't see that letter anywhere. I didn't feel right looking for it and left after a few minutes.

Mom had told Sandy and me to make spaghetti sauce for the first night out and showed us a recipe. Sandy started chopping onions while I put the meat in the big cast-iron skillet. I could hear her muttering, "Stupid onions," over the sound of the meat sizzling.

When I looked over, she'd stuck her knife right through the center of a huge onion and was whacking it on the cutting board.

"Hey!" I said. "That's not right. Just lay it down and cut it up."

"It doesn't work. I tried," she said, keeping right on whacking. The knife broke through the onion, and that onion sailed through the air and hit Barnabas, who was on his way into the kitchen.

He looked at us both standing there with our mouths open. He laughed, picked up the onion, and handed it to us. *"Ninyi ni wapishi wafundi,"* he said and laughed again.

That means, "You two are expert cooks."

We both laughed. Barnabas is great. He got something out of one of the cupboards and left again before I could think of a good answer.

"I know, we should get him to help us," Sandy said as soon as he had left.

"No way. Mom probably told him other stuff to do. It'd be cheating to get Barnabas to do this when we're supposed to do it. Here, I'll do the onions," I said, taking the knife from Sandy. "See, first you have to get the skin off," I said, picking at the papery layer. It just kept breaking apart, and the next layer down was kind of like skin too. Finally I just peeled off the whole outside ring.

"It wastes onion but at least it works," I muttered furiously. My eyes were starting to hurt and water. Without thinking, I rubbed them with my oniony hand.

"Ow!" I yelled, running for the sink.

"The meat's burning," Sandy cried. "What do I do?"

"Stir it!" I hollered, frantically splashing my stinging eyes with cold water.

"It's stuck to the bottom. I can't!"

I ran for the stove and grabbed the handle of the big skillet. "Ow!" I yelled again, jerking my hand back.

The skillet teetered on the edge of the stove. I yanked the handle of the drawer that held hot pads, and the whole drawer fell out on the floor with a crash.

"Anikaaa!" Sandy yelled.

"Why didn't you stir the meat before?" I snapped, picking up a hot pad and moving the big skillet to a safer place.

"You never said to," she protested. "Besides, I didn't ask you to do the onions."

"OK, you do them then," I said and started scraping furiously at the meat stuck to the bottom of the pan.

Sandy did get the onions chopped into chunks, more or less. They looked odd floating around in there with the tomatoes. I wondered if we were supposed to fry them first.

"Gross!" Sandy said, staring into the skillet. "I'm not eating this."

"It smells OK," I said hopefully and put a lid on it. I felt like I'd been doing the same thing with my worry about that letter. If I just sort of put a lid on it and left it alone, maybe it would come out OK.

"Whew!" Daddy said the next morning, slamming the trunk of the car shut. "I can't believe you all are going to pack all of this up the mountain."

"Not all of it!" I said, handing him the camera case. We were almost finished loading the car to leave. Mom had said we were going to carry our own packs. I'd never done that before. I shrugged my shoulders uneasily.

"See you in Nairobi!" Lisa yelled as we pulled out. Nairobi is Kenya's capital and quite a big city. Mom was very quiet during the hour-long drive. Daddy reached out to hold her hand.

We stopped at the mission guest house to pick up

jackets. Sandy and I found the jackets and started trying them on while Mom and Daddy were talking. Sandy found a jacket that fit her, but nothing fit me.

"You'll have to stay at the lodge with Daddy!" she taunted.

"I will not!" I protested. "I'll figure out something."

When we came out, Daddy was still talking. Usually Mom would have been the one to check and see that we both had jackets that fit us, but she was sitting staring into space and never asked. When Sandy started to tell her, I shushed her.

Mom, Sandy, and I went over to the African market while Daddy went to the bank. The inside of the huge, high-roofed building smelled of flowers and vegetables, raw meat and blood from the butchers, sweaty people, disinfectant, dirt, and spicy wood chips and wax from the wood carvers.

Usually I loved the noise and color, but this time I was too busy trying to figure out how to get a jacket without bothering Mom. Maybe Daddy would have an idea.

When we got back to the bank, Daddy was outside waiting for us.

"This is our lucky day," Mom said as she slid over to let Daddy drive. "It's an ocrediful incurance to get—"

"A what?!" Dad interrupted laughing.

"An ocrediful incurance," Sandy said, giggling.

"Leave me be," Mom said indignantly. "You know perfectly well what I mean. You almost never get your bank transaction taken care of that quickly."

"I agree absolutely," Dad said, still grinning. "Long live ocrediful incurances. May we meet with many of them."

When we actually found a parking place right next to the New Stanley Hotel, where we were supposed to meet the others, Sandy yelled, "Another ocrediful incurance!"

Even Mom laughed that time.

"We're off!" bellowed Uncle Joey as soon as he saw us. "Anika, you're coming with us! Lisa wants to ride with you."

Traci ran over to our car. I hung back trying to get a chance to tell Daddy I didn't have a jacket before we left Nairobi. Uncle Joey bellowed at me again.

"Anika, what's with you?" Daddy asked. "Move!"

Chapter
Three

"What were you guys laughing about so hard when you met us?" Lisa asked as I got into the car with her.

"It's my mom," I answered, only half paying attention. "She said it was an ocrediful incurance."

"What?" Lisa asked.

"See, it was especially good that Daddy got done early so we could get the other stuff done—"

I stopped and sat there feeling sick. It wasn't fair. This should be a great day, and now something was wrong with Mom, and maybe our whole family, and I didn't even have a jacket to wear for the climb.

Lisa poked me. "Anika, what's with you?"

I shrugged and ducked my head, then blurted out the easiest part to talk about. "We were supposed to find a jacket for me to wear on the mountain," I said, twisting to face her. "We never did. I can't climb without a jacket."

"Oh," Lisa said, and she was quiet for a moment. Then she said, "You can use mine."

"Are you sure?" I asked. "I thought you wanted to climb more now."

She shrugged and said, "Kind of, but it's not like it's a big deal."

"You're the best friend ever!" I said and hugged her. When I did, I ended up looking right at the back of Uncle Joey's head.

"Your dad—I bet your dad won't let you."

We both stopped and looked at him. Uncle Joey was talking a mile a minute to Uncle Paul and not paying any attention to us.

"Now the scree," he was saying. "Mark Jeremias said that was about the toughest part. But I figure it's just plain old will power, the old mind over matter—"

"Dad," Lisa interrupted.

He didn't even pause. "We'll just keep right on trucking no matter what—"

"Dad!" Lisa said, a bit louder.

"And beat that mountain—"

"Dad!!" Lisa yelled.

"What is it?" Uncle Joey said. "You don't need to yell at me."

Lisa gave me a quick look behind his back and rolled her eyes. Then she said, "Look, Anika doesn't have a jacket. Can I lend her mine and just stay at the lodge with Uncle Kevin?"

"Absolutely not!" Uncle Joey said. "I put myself on the line to give you this chance. I'm not going to have you miss out."

"Dad!" Lisa protested.

I felt relieved and worried at the same time. I hadn't felt really right about taking her jacket. But I wished Uncle Joey would be nicer to Lisa.

"I think there are jackets to rent at the lodge," Uncle Paul said suddenly.

I saw a flash of hope. I'd brought the money I had left from my birthday. Maybe it would be enough to rent a jacket, and I could do that without bothering Mom.

"Hey, look, there's the mountain!" Uncle Joey bellowed.

I scooted over against Lisa to see out her window better, and there it was. Still far away, the graceful shape of Mount Kenya's three jagged peaks showed above a layer of cloud. My breath caught in my throat.

I will get there, I will! I promised myself, staring at the peaks.

"Move over," Lisa hissed, elbowing me in the ribs.

I jumped and jerked back into my place.

"The mountain where the god lives," Uncle Paul said suddenly in a flat voice.

"Yeah, that's right. The Kikuyu thought that a god lived there, didn't they?" Uncle Joey said, laughing.

"Don't laugh. They knew that fierce spirits guarded the mountain," Uncle Paul said.

"Demons?" Lisa squeaked.

"That's right." I could see the little grin under Uncle Paul's big red beard, but Lisa couldn't. "Terrible, invisible demons that hurt hands and feet and made them stiff."

"I'm not climbing where there's any demons!" Lisa said.

Suddenly Uncle Joey bellowed with laughter. "I get it! It was just the cold. They'd never been in freezing weather. Their hands got cold and stiff."

"That's not demons," Lisa said indignantly.

"It wasn't just the cold," Uncle Paul said. "They had to gasp for breath. Sometimes their lungs filled up, and they choked and died. Then there were strange rocks that burned their hands, then turned to water when they tried to take them home."

"Ice!" I said, remembering how the snow in the Rocky Mountains had hurt the skin on my wrists and face when I fell skiing.

"And pulmonary edema from high altitude," Uncle Joey added triumphantly.

"So stop trying to scare me with demons!" Lisa said, still sounding angry and scared. "The mountain isn't guarded by demons! Besides, Jesus is stronger than demons anyway."

Uncle Joey bellowed with laughter, and twisted in his seat to poke Lisa. "You tell 'em," he said. "You're a tough kid. You and me, we'll show that mountain."

Lisa frowned. She pushed herself into the corner of the back seat, crossing her arms.

I glanced at her uneasily, then looked past her at the faraway mountain. Maybe there weren't demons, but except for that time skiing, I didn't remember being where it was seriously cold. I wasn't really any better off than the Kikuyu had been, and I didn't even have a jacket yet.

At Forest Lodge, while the adults were registering, I looked around for the place to rent things Uncle Paul talked about. There was a door off into a kind of shop.

I ducked my head. Someone was standing in the door staring at us. He gave me a funny feeling, like I ought to know him. I glanced up at him again, and he suddenly focused on just me. His eyes were very blue, and fierce.

"Come on," I whispered. Grabbing Lisa's arm, I pulled her with me around to the other side of the grown-ups.

"What's with you?" she asked.

"Didn't you see that guy by the door staring at us?" I demanded.

"Which guy?" she asked, and she stepped around so

she could see. I watched her, half holding my breath. That guy had given me such a weird feeling. She looked back at me, shrugged, and put one eyebrow up, like I was crazy. I stepped out after her. There was no one there.

"He *was* there!" I said indignantly.

"It must be the high altitude affecting your brain already," Lisa said, laughing.

"He was there," I repeated. "He had dark hair, and these really blue, fierce eyes."

"She's in love," Lisa said, giggling even harder. "Hey Traci, Sandy, Anika's in love."

"Oh, shut up!" I said, but I was grinning too. Lisa's laugh is like that.

Mom's voice rescued me. "Come on, kids. We've got to go get moved in."

Instead of following them, I dodged into the shop where you rent stuff.

"We have no children's jackets," the man in charge said, shrugging and showing empty hands. It turned out that a ladies' small fit me pretty good, though.

He named a price that was only ten shillings more than I had. You can almost always bargain in Kenya, so I tried, and he finally did let me have it for all the money I had.

I ran out and skipped across the parking lot toward our car, hugging the jacket. It was heavy, and the outside felt like canvas. I smiled. The cold demons couldn't get me in this jacket.

"Thanks, God," I said softly and then yelled across the empty parking lot, "Watch out, cold demons—here I come!"

Daddy stood up from the other side of the car. "What was that, Anika?"

"Um, nothing, Daddy," I said, feeling my face get hot. "What can I carry?"

He pointed, and I grabbed the cooler and started off.

"It's the first little cabin on the left," Daddy called after me.

I hitched the cooler up to get a better grip and looked around for the first time since we got there. The sun was low in the sky and lit the lawns and flowers with a golden glow. Everything was green and lush. A cool breeze lifted my hair.

I spun around to see everything. The cooler swung out and pulled hard on my hands.

Then I got a shock that knocked the smile right off my face. That same guy I'd seen by the shop had stepped into the path right in front of me. I stopped with a jerk that made the cooler slam into my stomach, then tried to dodge around him. At first he wouldn't let me. He just stood in the way staring at me like I was a ghost. Finally he let me go.

What's with him? I wondered, walking away fast. *Why does he make me feel odd, like I ought to know him?* When I thought I was a safe distance away, I looked back. He was still standing in the path, staring after me.

"Did you see him?" Sandy asked me as soon as I came up to them.

Sandy, Traci, and Lisa were outside between the two tiny cabins that we were going to stay in that night.

I nodded, putting the cooler down on the grass and dumping my new jacket on top of it.

"Was he the same one—?" Lisa began.

Sandy interrupted, sounding angry. "He was standing right by the path, and he kept staring and staring at us."

"Yeah, is it your boyfriend?" asked Traci.

"Yes—I mean, *no* he isn't my boyfriend," I said, shaking my head. "It's the same guy I saw before, only this time he stood right in my way and wouldn't let me get past."

"Tell your boyfriend to go away," Traci said. "I don't want to go back for more stuff if he's still there."

"He is *not* my boyfriend," I yelled.

Uncle Joey's voice boomed out of one of the cabins. "Hey, we all know you're boy crazy already. Leave off about the boys and go get more gear!"

"But Uncle Joey, there's this—," Traci started.

Uncle Joey burst out of the cabin and started shooing us down the path like chickens.

That guy wasn't around where we could see him. When we got back, Daddy was setting up the camp stove outside our cabin.

"Sandy! Anika! Come here," Mom called from our cabin. "We've got to organize our packs."

"You too, Traci," Uncle Paul called from the other cabin.

Our family was in one cabin; Traci, Lisa, and their dads were in the other.

When I turned to go in, Sandy grabbed at me. I jerked away from her and hissed, "What?"

"Daddy's cooking the spaghetti," she whispered and made a small pointing movement that Daddy wouldn't see.

I looked back. Outside between the cabins, Daddy had set up the little camping stove. He was just putting the spaghetti pot on.

"Did you taste it to see if it was OK after it cooked?" Sandy asked.

"No . . . did you?" I asked. She just shook her head.

Burnt-meat-and-onion-lump spaghetti—yuck. Now we're in for it, I thought, heading into the cabin.

"We decided that you kids just need to carry your own sleeping bags and clothes," Mom said as we walked in. "Uncle Joey, Uncle Paul, and I will carry the food and the rest of the gear. Lay all your stuff out on the bed first and then—Anika, where did you get that jacket?"

I ducked my head. "I rented it at the lodge with my birthday money," I said. "There wasn't one that fit me at Mayfair, and I didn't want to bug you."

There was a small, uncomfortable silence. I held my breath, wondering if she'd ask why I didn't want to bug her. I dreaded it, but at least it would get whatever was wrong out in the open. She didn't ask.

She just said, "Good idea," and kept talking about packing up.

I sighed and started putting things into the pack Mom handed me. Its rough sides slid up past my arms. The ugly gray-brown pack looked tough and carried scuff marks and mended spots from other people's adventures. *Now it's my turn,* I thought and felt a bit better.

My sleeping bag was supposed to go into a round duffel space right at the bottom of the pack. It didn't want to fit. I was shoving away at it with my teeth clenched when Daddy called, "Supper!"

Sandy and I looked at each other and didn't move.

A second later Traci burst in the door. "Come on, Sandy, it's supper. Did you get all your stuff in your pack?" She grabbed Sandy's pack. "Hey, it's heavier than mine."

Lisa came in just then.

"Is my pack heavier than yours?" I asked, wanting to keep up the distraction from supper.

Lisa gave me a funny look, but she lifted it to see, then nodded.

"I know," Sandy said. "It's those stupid green ponchos Mom got. They weigh a ton."

"Maybe you can get her to let you leave them," Lisa said, looking at me. "My dad said it won't rain anyway."

"Don't you guys have any—?" I started to ask, but Daddy's voice cut me off.

"Girls, get out here. Now!"

It was no use delaying any longer. Right after Uncle Joey said grace, Mom said, "I'd just like to let you know Anika and Sandy made this spaghetti sauce for us."

I cringed.

"Hey, is that so?" Uncle Joey boomed. He held out his plate. "Fill her up, and I'll check it out." Grinning at us, he took a huge bite. I glanced at Sandy, who had her head down, then back at Uncle Joey.

He swallowed and bellowed, "It's good! You two are hired as expedition cooks."

I let out my breath with a *whoosh* and got into line to get my food. I stirred that sauce for a second before I took mine. The onions had disappeared.

"Maybe Mom made different sauce and didn't say," Sandy whispered.

"No, I didn't," Mom answered from right behind me. "Why? What's wrong with it?" she asked.

"Well, Anika kind of burned the meat," Sandy said.

"And Sandy put in these huge chunks of onion. They were floating around in there like dead fish with their white bellies up."

"They weren't that bad!" Sandy protested.

Mom laughed. "And you've been worried ever since we left home? The sauce was fine by the time it cooked a couple of hours. Onions disappear if they're cooked long enough. The dark browned meat just gave it a good flavor."

"Oh," I said, feeling dumb, and ladled a big glob of sauce onto my spaghetti noodles.

"You've been up here before, Paul. What are we in for tomorrow?" Uncle Joey asked.

I stopped chewing to listen, but Uncle Paul is never in a hurry to talk.

"Well, there's the rain forest," he said after a long pause. "After that there's the vertical bog, and finally a long walk through the Teliki Valley."

"Is any of it likely to give us trouble?" Mom asked.

Uncle Paul looked at her, then methodically ate another mouthful. Halfway through he nodded at Sandy and me and made an OK sign to say the spaghetti was good. I squirmed, wishing he'd hurry.

"The vertical bog can be vicious, and of course we don't know how the kids will do carrying packs." He paused. "I guess a lot of it depends on the weather. If it rains hard, the road up to the top of the forest becomes impassable to vehicles. The vertical bog gets softer from the runoff, and the snow gets deep and soft on the last stretch to the top of Lanana."

"They told me it doesn't rain this time of year," Uncle Joey said, sounding indignant.

Uncle Paul just raised his eyebrows, tipped his head sideways, and took another bite. I wondered if he was laughing at Uncle Joey.

My stomach knotted. It was near the end of the dry season. It could rain. Suddenly I wasn't very hungry. I just had to make it. No matter what, in spite of this thing with Mom, I just had to.

"Only God knows what the weather will do." Daddy said. "You asked me to lead devotions. I'd like to read Psalm 121. It seems appropriate."

I'd heard the psalm before, but this time was different. Daddy's soft, deep voice carried across the dusk under the trees.

"'I look up to the hills. But where does my help come from? My help comes from the Lord. He made heaven and earth. He will not let you be defeated. He who guards you never sleeps. He who guards Israel never rests or sleeps. The Lord guards you. The Lord protects you as the shade protects you from the sun. The sun cannot hurt you during the day. And the moon cannot hurt you at night. The Lord will guard you from all dangers. He will guard your life. The Lord will guard you as you come and go, both now and forever.'"

As I snuggled into my sleeping bag on the top bunk, I thought about the psalm. *"My help comes from the Lord. He made heaven and earth."* I thought, *That fits with what I read before about the Father giving us strength out of his great glory.*

The sound of rain rattling on the tin roof woke me up in the middle of the night. It was pouring outside.

I lay there stiff as a board trying to make it stop raining. *Please God, stop the rain, stop the rain, stop the rain,* ran over and over through my head.

"Kevin, are you awake?" Mom asked suddenly in a soft voice.

"Umhum," Daddy answered.

"Since I got the letter I can't get him out of my head. He said his name is Rick."

"Hazel, it will be OK," Daddy muttered, still sounding sleepy.

"It isn't OK." Her voice sounded tense. "It's horrible realizing I don't know anything about my own child. He's almost an adult. This could ruin our family."

Ruin our family? What did she mean? Her own child? Sandy and I are her only kids. She was talking about the same letter that made her cry. Who is Rick, anyway? I got goosebumps all over my body. I held absolutely still.

"Look," Daddy said. "We've prayed for the child ever since we came to the Lord. You'll just have to leave it in his hands."

"But the girls . . . ," Mom said, sounding desperate.

The springs creaked, and I could hear Daddy going over to Mom. Then things were quiet.

I lay still, thinking hard. Nothing made sense. Mom couldn't have another kid, could she? An older one she didn't know? It didn't make sense. After a long time, I finally went back to sleep.

Chapter Four

The sun was shining, sparkling on wet grass, when I woke up.

I settled my pack onto my back for the walk to the car. Daddy was going to drive us as far as he could go in the car. My pack felt good. Not heavy at all. What I'd heard in the night seemed far away. Like a dream. Today was real. Climbing the mountain was real. I took a deep breath and trotted up the path to catch up with Lisa.

"Wow!" Lisa said, stopping. "Look!"

Mount Kenya was clear of the clouds and looming over us above the trees. The snow shone pure white against a deep blue sky.

"Glorious, isn't it?" Daddy said, coming up behind us. "It almost makes me wish I was climbing. Almost, but not quite. I saw some nice rises on the creek already this morning. You can think of me while you're struggling in the bog."

"But Daddy, look at it! How can you not want to climb? I'd want to try even if there were three vertical bogs."

He grinned and said, "Keep that determination. You'll need it."

Pretty soon we were all jammed into our car, eight people and seven packs. Sandy's skinny behind bit into my knees as the car swayed and slithered in the mud.

"Paul, this is pretty slick," Daddy said as he twisted the wheel to correct a skid. A few seconds later we slid to a stop. I hunched over, trying to see out past Sandy's head.

"Ow! Anika, hold still!" Lisa exclaimed. "Your elbow is killing my ribs."

"What's happening?" I asked.

"It's the park gate," Traci answered.

"Everybody out!" Daddy said.

The adults went into the wooden building, but we stayed outside on the porch. I leaned against the rail, watching the mountain through the gray veil of cloud that had started blowing across the peaks. My throat was tight with wanting to be there, up on the top. Just for a second the two top peaks shone clear. Then they were gone. I waited, staring at the place.

"Anika! Hey, Anika!"

I spun around and came over to join the others.

"You all have a decision to make," Daddy said. "The rangers said that the road isn't passable for much further."

"I'm ready for a hike," Uncle Joey said, throwing his head back. "So what if it's a bit longer."

"You kids are sure about this?" Mom asked. "It could add as much as four hours to an already difficult hike."

I nodded, and so did Sandy and Traci.

"Lisa?" Mom asked.

"No kid of mine is going to wimp out!" Uncle Joey bellowed, thumping her on the back.

Mom kept waiting for Lisa to answer.

She looked down for a moment and then said, "Um-hm. I guess."

Uncle Paul had been watching with thoughtful eyes. Now he said, "Before you kids decide, read this."

He handed us each a pink paper. I read the first few lines. It was some park thing about rules. I dropped it and said, "I'm ready!"

Uncle Paul bent down and picked my paper off the muddy porch floor. "Read it," he said in a voice that was almost a growl.

My face felt hot, and I ducked my head to read.

I started reading the next part and almost stopped breathing. It said if we got off the path and got lost, we could die of overexposure. It said your lungs could fill up and your heart stop from the high altitude. It said to bring anybody down right away whose breathing got rough. It talked about headaches and throwing up. Then it said that many people climb safely every year, and to be safe and enjoy our climb.

44

I swallowed hard and looked up. Daddy was watching me. "You can always come fish with me," he said.

"No way!" I said.

The other kids agreed, even Lisa.

"Let's all pray together before we start," Mom said.

All I said for my prayer was, "Dear God, please keep us safe and please help us to get to the top of your mountain." I didn't even want to think about what I'd heard Mom say in the night.

"OK," Daddy said, looking up at the end. "Let's see how far I can get you with the car. All aboard!"

I looked up one more time at the cloud that hid the mountain, and I climbed into the car.

"Move over," Lisa said as she climbed in.

"I can't," I said. "There's no more room. Ow! Sandy, move your rear."

"Everybody in?" Mom asked, looking back over her shoulder. "Hold on tight. This could get rough."

The car lurched and swayed steadily up the road. Blobs of reddish-brown mud hit the windows. The engine growled in low gear.

"At least we got farther than some people," Lisa said, pointing out the window. I craned my head to see.

"Ow! Hold still!" Sandy snapped. "It's just a parked car with a guy getting out with a pack."

"Hey! It's that same guy!" Traci said.

45

"Is not!"

"Is too. Your boyfriend is climbing, Anika. Maybe you'll get to see him."

"He is *not* my—"

The car swung hard to the left, and Sandy's head whacked me in the mouth. I could hear the wheels spinning as we skidded toward the ditch. The car stopped.

Rrrrrrr! Rrrrrrrr! The car swayed as Daddy gunned the engine rhythmically a couple of times. We didn't budge. He put it in reverse, and we moved.

"Duck your heads, kids. I've got to see to back up," he said over his shoulder.

We bumped back downhill a ways, then he took another run at the muddy spot. Fishtailing and jerking, we made it through. A few seconds later we were stuck again. This time going backwards didn't help.

"We're hoofing it from here," Uncle Joey said. "This is it. Move it, kids."

We unloaded all the packs and stacked them on the side of the road, out of the mud. Then we had to push the car. Uncle Joey got right behind one of the back wheels to push. The wheel kicked up a huge glob of mud that hit his face. His eyes looked like white buttons on a brown shirt.

For a second we just stared. Then Sandy giggled, and we all laughed, even Uncle Joey.

When we quit laughing, he raised his arms in a big shrug and said, "Who wants to be clean when we're roughing it?" He got down to push again. A few seconds later the car was out and turned around.

Daddy couldn't stop without getting stuck again. He waved out the window and yelled, "God go with you!" Then he was gone.

It was suddenly quiet. There was no wind. I could hear water dripping off the tall bamboo along the road. I looked at the gray-green woods and smiled. This was it. We were actually climbing Mount Kenya.

"Make sure your rain gear is on top," Mom said as she picked up her pack.

I shoved my hand down the side of my pack, feeling for the slick rubber of the poncho. I was jerking it out when I looked up at Lisa. She'd already put her pack on her shoulders.

"Don't you have rain gear?" I asked.

She shrugged and looked worried. "Dad said it isn't going to rain."

"You hope," I said. I got my pack on awkwardly, and Lisa and I started up the road.

We walked ahead of the others. The road was slick, and I was glad for mud boots. Lisa's shoes were already soaked and muddy. There were huge cedar trees by the road with long trailers of gray-green moss dangling from their trunks and branches. Some of their trunks looked like something had twisted them round and round.

"Uncle Paul, how come the trees are like that?" I heard Sandy ask.

I couldn't hear his quiet answer—they were too far behind us—but I heard Traci's, "Daaad, there's no such thing as mountain giants who twist trees."

Uncle Joey's laugh echoed off the far side of the ravine we were following. "Good one, Paul! Mountain giants!"

He was interrupted by loud crashing in the bamboo off to the right of the road. Sandy screamed. I froze and Lisa grabbed me hard, hurting my arm.

The crashing moved away from us. Lisa dragged me back to the others.

"No giants, huh?" Uncle Paul said, grinning in his beard.

"It wasn't!" Traci insisted, still shaking. "It was elephants or buffalo or something, and they don't twist trees!"

Everybody laughed, and we kept on walking. Lisa wouldn't walk very far in front now.

We didn't talk much. Walking up the steep, slippery road took all our breath. Our feet made soft sucking sounds in the mud. We came around a corner and saw what looked like a painted picture. Three bushbuck stood frozen in a tiny meadow by the road. Lisa and I held still without breathing. There were two does, red against the green grass, and a larger, darker buck. Their heads were turned towards us with big ears like satellite dishes listening.

Uncle Paul came up behind us and stood still too. Then Uncle Joey came around the corner.

"Hey, kids!" he bellowed back at Traci and Sandy. "Look at this."

The bushbuck were gone in a flash.

"Oops, sorry. Heh heh!" he said. We just looked at each other.

Later Uncle Paul spotted some buffalo. Dark patches of hide showed through breaks in the bush across the ravine. We stopped to rest and watch them. When we held still, we could hear them moving through the bush.

"Look!" Traci said. She wasn't looking at the buffalo. She was looking back down the road. The guy who'd been staring at us at the lodge was hiking towards us. I ducked my head while he passed.

"Did you see how he stared at your mom?" Lisa asked me softly.

I shook my head. Who was he, anyway?

Later we passed a bridge with a sign that said, "Elephants have the right of way." That reminded Mom of a true story about a woman who'd been climbing. The woman wanted to go back and didn't want to make her friends stop, so she started walking back down to the car alone. She came around a corner, and a whole herd of big black cape buffalo were on the road. Without thinking, she dove over the edge of the steep bank into the top of a tree. All the buffalo did was run away. She had to wait in the tree until somebody came to help get her out.

We all laughed, but I wondered if I wouldn't have done the same thing.

At the end of the road we came up out of the trees into a misty grassland. In the grass, the path split and became twenty paths braided together around hairy humps of grass. Alongside were twisted bushes twice as tall as people. Gray wisps of cloud were blowing by.

Sandy and Traci were going slower and slower. Mom stayed with them. Uncle Paul called a halt to wait for them. I flopped down on the grass tufts and sighed. I was tired and my left heel was starting to hurt.

"What are these tree things?" Uncle Joey demanded, pointing at the weird bushes. He looked indignant, like he thought such things shouldn't exist.

"Giant heather," Uncle Paul answered.

"What!" Uncle Joey said. "Giant heather?"

Uncle Paul smiled in his beard and said, "God put things here you won't find anywhere else on earth."

Listening to Uncle Paul made me feel good. I looked at the odd giant heather plants, and it seemed like God had made them just to have fun.

"Gnome plants! We'll see gnome plants," I said suddenly, remembering a picture book of Kenya's mountains that I'd seen at school. "They look just like hairy people."

Both men stared at me. I ducked my head, thinking, *The book did say that!*

By the time Mom and the other kids caught up, I was ready to go. It made me impatient to have to wait while they rested.

An hour later we hit the vertical bog. It wasn't exactly vertical, but it was more than steep enough for me. Between tough, wiry clumps of grass were deep patches of mud. The ground was full of springs. There was a fine mist falling that made everything soaking wet. Shining drops of water lined every blade of grass, making the whole world look silver.

It looked pretty, but it didn't feel pretty. No matter how carefully I tried to keep my balance, I kept falling. I'd step over a high clump of grass onto what looked like firm ground only to go into knee-deep, cold, black mud. Other times my foot would hit one of the big gray lumps of rock, making my teeth snap together from the jar it gave me.

It seemed to go on forever. I got wetter and wetter. Each time I had to struggle out of a mudhole it was harder. My soaked pants were cold and heavy, and my hands felt stiff and swollen from being wet and cold.

Whack. My pack thudded into my back as my foot hit another unexpected rock. I shoved my pack back into place and grimly stepped over the next clump of grass. Nothing fit into my head now but the need to keep going. I wasn't paying attention to where Lisa was, or Mom or anybody.

"Never!" I muttered to myself, catching my balance at the edge of another mudhole. "I won't quit!" I scrambled and slid over another huge clump of wiry, slippery grass. "The bog can't last forever!" I whispered, picking myself up again.

It seemed like it did. My mind was totally numb. I ended up muttering, "Never . . . forever . . . never . . . forever . . . ," as I struggled.

Each time I slipped, the pack thudded into my back or jerked me sideways. The straps bit into my shoulders and hurt. I shrugged and tried to shift them, but they always came back to the same sore spot.

I stepped over a huge hummock of grass, missed my footing in the mud, and barely kept myself from falling again. I gritted my teeth and kept going. "Never . . . forever . . . never . . . forever . . ."

My left heel ached where the rubber boot rubbed it. I fell again, splashing myself with icy water from a puddle. I grabbed the tough grass and hauled myself up.

"Anika! Aniiiikaa!" Somebody was calling my name. "Anika! Stop!"

I swung around and looked back. Everybody was in a group at least a hundred yards behind me. I hadn't realized that I'd gotten in front. Well, I wasn't going back only to have to climb up again. That was for sure. I'd just wait here.

I sat down with a plop and leaned my pack against one of the big gray boulders that stuck up out of the rough grass like teeth. It felt unbelievably wonderful to hold still. I lay there like I was dead, looking up at the misty sky. Mom called again, but I didn't move.

After a bit I sat up and looked at the others. They were passing around a canteen and something to eat. Suddenly my stomach felt hollow and I noticed how thirsty I was. But I still wasn't going to go down.

I looked around. Blowing wisps of cloud cut off the view. Every now and then there'd be a ragged rip in the clouds. Through a rip in the cloud I saw land, far down away from us, looking milky brown and patchy. I turned to look the other way to see if I could see the peaks.

I saw him! It was the same guy. He was sitting against a gray boulder staring at me. The others couldn't see him because of the rock. Suddenly I was mad. Why couldn't he leave us alone? I dumped my pack, got up, and marched towards him, stumbling over the slippery grass.

He watched me coming without moving.

I stopped about five feet from him, jammed my hands on my hips, and demanded, "Who do you think you are, anyway? Why don't you leave me alone!"

He frowned and shook his head. Finally he asked, "Your name is Anika Scott, right?"

I nodded without thinking. Then shock went through me like cold water down the neck. How did he know my name? I clenched my teeth and said, "So?"

"Tell your mom for me that Rick wants to talk to her," he said. Without waiting for an answer he picked up his pack and walked off.

Chapter
Five

I stared after him with my mouth open. He strode up the slope without stopping. Rick? Wasn't that the name Mom had said in the night? Did this guy who kept staring at us have something to do with the letter?

I shook myself and started to walk back to the path, not really paying attention to where I was going. My foot slipped on a tuft of grass, and I sat down hard. I got up still thinking about what the guy had said and stumbled on.

Should I tell Mom what he said? Was he the same Rick? If he was, and if what I'd thought about was right, then he'd be my—

"No!" I yelled right out loud. "No! No! That's stupid! It's not true!"

I missed my footing and sat down hard again. The guy had said Rick wanted to talk to Mom. Did he mean himself? That was stupid. How could the same Rick be here? Even if he did exist, which he *didn't,* he'd be in the States.

I shook my head to clear it and looked around. A wave of fear made my stomach get tight. I couldn't see the path, or my pack, or Mom and the others. I looked back. My stomach hurt worse. I couldn't tell which jagged, gray-black boulder was the one I'd just come from.

I swallowed hard and spun in a circle looking. I could hear my heart beat in my ears. I was lost! I could die! I chose a direction and started to walk. Nothing changed but the shapes of the boulders—no path, no people. I started to run and fell over one of the hard, slippery clumps of grass.

It wasn't any use. Tears stung my eyes. I couldn't hold them back. After a long time I couldn't cry any more. My mouth tasted like old metal, and my eyes ached. After a bit I sat up. My shirt was cold and wet from the clump of grass I'd been sprawled over.

I hugged myself to get warm, and whispered, "Please help me from your strength, God. I'm scared."

I shivered and hugged my knees tighter. I was in the bottom of a slanted dip in the land. *Maybe if I go to the top and climb up one of those boulders I could see something,* I thought, and shivered harder. Anything was better than just sitting.

I frowned and tried to think clearly. I didn't even know which way I'd been going when I fell. Tears stung my eyes again, but I blinked them back furiously.

Please let me choose the right way to go, I prayed. *In Jesus' name, amen.*

I picked a tall boulder that looked like I could climb it and started to hike toward it. It was farther than I thought, but the ground was dryer. At least I was out of the bog. I kept on going. When I finally got there and touched its rough, cold, wet side, I was too tired to climb. My foot was hurting badly where the boot rubbed my heel. I leaned my head against the cold rock.

Suddenly I held my breath. Was that voices? I listened hard. Yes, it was—people talking far off. Maybe Mom and everybody, or just other people on the path.

I got a good grip on a knob with my hand and frantically started to climb. It was steep and slippery. I banged my knee hard partway up and almost fell. After that I was more careful. On top, I balanced myself and stood up.

All around me was a wide sweep of lumpy, misty grassland. The boulders stood like ancient Druid stones, and mist blew by. I could see no people, hear no voices. I sank back down onto the rock and hid my face. The wind cut through my wet clothes, making my teeth chatter.

I picked up my head and looked around again. A grayish brown thing lying in a hollow in the grass a ways off caught my eye. I stared at it blankly at first. Gradually I started wondering what it was. Finally I stood up to see better.

It looked like canvas. A backpack? I stared harder, shut my eyes, and opened them again to see better. It was the same color as my pack—*my pack!* My pack where I'd left it by the trail!

I turned and slithered off that rock, hit a bump, and fell the last seven feet with a thud. I jumped back out of the mud and stared. I couldn't see the pack anymore. I ran two steps then stopped and thought. The pack was in a hollow. I could go right by it without seeing it. Besides, I wasn't absolutely sure that I was going exactly the right direction.

I sighed and went back to the rock. The climb to the top seemed harder this time. At first I couldn't see the pack, then there it was. Carefully I looked at the spot where it was, memorized the shape of the clumps of grass. Then I made a line in my head from the pack to my rock and picked things along the way.

"OK," I muttered to myself as I climbed down. "First I'll go to the rock shaped like a big suitcase, then the soggy little pond. After that is the rock that's split in the middle, and if I stand on that I should be able to see the pack."

The first part was easy. I got to the rock shaped like a suitcase, but I couldn't see the pond—not even when I climbed on top of the rock. I was going to start walking in what I hoped was the right direction when I stopped again. Maybe I could see the split rock. I stopped and looked and looked, and there it was. It didn't look the same exactly, but when I looked close I recognized the way it had an especially big clump of grass at one end.

I set off at a run, stumbling, slipping, and falling. Frantically I scrambled up the rock, jamming my feet into the crack to get a grip. I couldn't see anything that looked like a pack. Taking a deep breath, I turned slowly around, looking. Nothing. My body went limp, and I sat down with a thump.

"Please, God, help me find it," I whispered. I swallowed hard and thought. *OK, what direction was it from the split rock? Sort of that way.* I pointed carefully and stood up to look again. There was something—a little tag of something sticking up.

I slid down off the rock and ran. After about twenty steps I skidded to a stop and stared at the ground. The path up the mountain was a bunch of beaten-down tracks all winding through the grass clumps. You couldn't see them unless you were standing right on them, and I *was!*

"Thank you, God!" I yelled at the top of my voice. I couldn't see the pack at all now, but I kept going. I tripped and slid facefirst into a hollow. There was my pack right beside me. I hugged it and lay there panting.

I climbed out to look back at where I'd left Mom and everybody. They weren't there!

Numb with fear and cold, I stood still. How could the others have left me?

"God, you got me back to the path like I asked, but it's no good. There's nobody here." My throat got tight, and I swallowed hard. A gust of wind cut through my clothes. With a noise like ripping cloth, rain swept across the grass. Ice-cold drops stung my cheeks.

I knelt by my pack and fumbled it open with thick, cold fingers. I pulled the heavy rubbery-smelling poncho over my head. The noise of the rain spattering on the rubber sounded incredibly loud as I struggled to get the poncho straight. Cold rubber on a wet shirt didn't make me warm. I dug for my jacket, trying to keep the pack under my poncho, and struggled into it. That was better. I crouched down beside the pack and used one flap of the poncho to cover it from the rain.

Hunched there under the poncho I tried to think. Where had the others gone, up the mountain or down? My eyebrows knotted with concentration. Maybe they went down because of the rain. Lisa didn't have a raincoat. They wouldn't just leave me, would they? Maybe they were going up and thought I'd gone on ahead.

I swallowed hard and hung my head. Rain dripped off the hood of my poncho, making a screen between me and the silver-gray grass. It was no use moving.

I chewed my knuckle, worrying. The taste of the water on my cold, wet hand reminded me of how thirsty I was. I bunched my poncho together so that the rain ran into a dip and tried to drink that. Most of it spilled down my neck.

I froze to listen. There were voices! The poncho sprayed water in all directions as I jumped wildly to my feet. Two men! There were two men coming down the path about a hundred yards ahead of me.

"Hey!" I yelled, waving wildly, and I ran towards them, stumbling because my legs were so cold.

As I ran to meet them I could see they were Japanese or Chinese or something. People come from all over to climb Mount Kenya.

"Did you see my mom? Did you pass them?" I blurted.

"Excuse, not understand much English," the shorter man said. "Please to say more slowly."

I took a deep breath and said slowly and clearly, "Did you pass two men, one woman, and three children going up the mountain? See, I got lost and now I don't know if they went—"

He held up his hand to stop me because I'd started talking faster and faster. The taller man said something to him in another language and he answered. Then he turned back to me.

"Yes, we see. Also they ask for girl. Are you girl?"

I nodded wildly, grabbed my pack by one strap, and started to run past them up the path.

The taller man yelled something, came after me, and grabbed my arm. His friend, who knew English, came panting up.

"Please to wait!" he exclaimed. "If hurry too much, not good. Slow will arrive in safety. Also must put pack on properly."

His friend took my pack and motioned me to take off my poncho. I grabbed to get the pack back and glared at him. Were they thieves?

The shorter man waved his hand back and forth. "Pack must not be rain," he said. "Can go under roof of coat." He motioned toward his friend, who spun around to show me his back. His pack was underneath the back flap of his poncho.

"Oh," I said, feeling silly, and let go of my pack. A couple of seconds later they'd helped me get my pack under my poncho properly.

"Thanks!" I said, and I started up the path, walking fast.

The short man called after me, "Girl! Please to remember slow."

My foot and the shoulder straps of the pack stung viciously. The pain faded to a bearable ache in a few minutes. I looked back. The men were out of sight. I started to run. I just had to catch Mom and the others.

My pack rode up and whacked me in the back of the head at every step. Water got down my neck because the poncho hood kept flopping off. My lungs ached and I gasped for breath like I was dying of asthma. I kept slipping and stumbling.

Finally I went down—hard. I just sat there gasping and sobbing. As soon as I could breathe I struggled to my feet and started walking. I was warmer, but my legs felt like rubber. *Running was a stupid idea,* I thought bitterly, as I stumbled over another grass clump. *Those men were right.*

"Anika!"

My head snapped up. Uncle Paul! Uncle Paul was coming down the path!

I yelled for joy and stumbled towards him. He grabbed me in a bear hug.

"Am I ever glad to see you!" He hugged me again and then stepped back. "Your mother is fit to be tied. When we lost sight of you we assumed you'd gone on ahead, but then those Chinese men hadn't seen you. Did you see them?"

I nodded.

"We had no idea where you were by that time. Joey has gone ahead to try to catch you on the path. Your mom and the kids are waiting, and I came back this way."

"Is everybody mad?" I whispered.

"You have some explaining to do," he said. "Look, I'll go ahead to tell your mother you're OK and try to catch Joey. You just keep on coming. See that ridge?" he asked, pointing ahead. "They're in a cave just over the top of that. OK?"

I nodded.

"Just make sure you stay on the path."

"I will!" I said fervently.

Uncle Paul looked at me hard, laughed, and said, "I guess you will." Then he waved and headed up the steep path at a fast, swinging walk. I tried to keep up, but I had to sit down and rest after a little way. Pretty soon he was out of sight.

It seemed ages before I came over the crest of that ridge. Just off the path there was a wide and low opening like a giant frog's mouth with black lips. Mom, Sandy, Traci, and Lisa were sitting just inside the cave.

Mom ran towards me and gave me a big hug. "Anika, what on earth happened? What yid you det surdelf into this time?" she demanded.

I laughed and hugged her hard, thinking, *My very own mom*. Suddenly I remembered why I'd got lost.

"Mom," I said, but she kept right on talking.

"My heart dropped when I looked up to where you'd been sitting and you were gone. Do you realize how much trouble you've put Uncle Paul and Uncle Joey through?!"

"I didn't mean to!" I insisted with my head down.

"Come on, let's get out of the rain," Mom said, heading for the cave. I followed her.

"What happened?" blurted Sandy as we ducked into the opening. "Where did you go?"

"It was that same guy," I said, looking at Mom. "That same guy that's been staring at us."

"What guy?" Mom asked.

"He has!" I said and looked at Sandy and Traci. "Right?"

They nodded, and Sandy said, "He got right in my way when I was carrying stuff to the cabin."

"Anyway," I interrupted, "when you stopped I saw that he was there watching us, off the path behind a rock where you couldn't see him."

I stopped and shuffled my feet in the thick gray dust on the cave floor.

"Did he kidnap you or something?" Traci demanded, sounding excited.

I gave her a disgusted look. "No." I gulped and plunged on. "It was weird. I went over and told him to leave us alone. He asked me if my name was Anika Scott, then—"

"Well?" Sandy and Traci both blurted.

Slowly I went on. "He said for me to tell my mother—" I paused and looked at her uneasily. "Tell you that Rick wants to talk to you."

Traci said, "Ha, ha, he must want to marry you! Anika has a boyfriend! Anika has a boyfriend."

"Shut up!" Sandy said, kicking her in the ankle. She was watching Mom the same as I was. Mom had gone sheet white. Her eyes were blank. She wandered vaguely over to a rock, sat down, and hung her head.

I felt sick. I spun on my heel and stood in the cave mouth with my back to her. *It can't be true! I won't let it!* I thought furiously.

Everything was dead quiet behind me. Then Mom asked, "Are you sure that's what he said, Anika? Rick wants to talk to me? Here in Kenya?" Her voice sounded shaky.

I nodded, then spun around and added fiercely, "He never said he was Rick."

She didn't answer. She was sitting still with her head in her hands. I wondered if she was praying.

"What's going on?" Traci asked uneasily.

Sandy whispered, "I don't know."

I turned to look at them and then looked away and bit my lip. My heart was pounding so hard I could hear it in my head. I wasn't going to tell them. I wasn't going to let it be true. I shook my head. It couldn't be. That guy Rick couldn't be Mom's kid. . . . I gulped and shoved the thought away. It was impossible. That would mean that Mom had—

"I see the lost sheep has returned!" Uncle Joey boomed, stamping his feet as he came into the cave. I nearly jumped out of my skin. He walloped me on the shoulder. "Scared ya, did I? Well, now we're even." He grabbed my elbows and spun me around to face him. "You had me scared, disappearing like that, Anika Scott." Then he grinned and squeezed my arms tighter, gave me a little shake and put me down. "Great to have you back."

By the time I caught my balance he'd left me. I glanced over at Mom. She was on her feet doing something with her pack. I couldn't see her face.

I was watching her so hard that what Uncle Joey was saying to Lisa didn't sink in for a few seconds.

". . . quit already?" He yelled so loud that it finally penetrated my brain. "Just because you got a little damp, you wimp out?"

I glanced over. Lisa was sitting huddled miserably on a rock. Her wet hair was plastered to her head. She ducked her head and didn't answer her father.

"She's not 'a little damp,' Joey. She's soaked, the same as you are," Uncle Paul said. He was silhouetted against the sky, standing in the mouth of the cave.

"So what's a little water?" Uncle Joey demanded. "Not enough to make *me* quit, I'll tell you right now."

That grabbed my attention. I stopped thinking about Rick. "Quit?" I blurted. "We're not quitting, are we?"

Chapter
Six

Everything was turning out horrible.

"No way!" Traci said. "Dad, you can't make us quit!"

"Mom!" Sandy demanded. "Mom! We're not going back, are we?"

Without turning around, Mom said in a low, tight voice, "I'll leave that up to Paul."

I spun to look at the two men. Uncle Paul was looking thoughtfully at Mom. His big red beard was beaded with water.

"Paul!" Uncle Joey said. "You're not going to let my wimp of a daughter ruin this for everyone!" His angry voice echoed and filled the cave.

I cringed and glanced at Lisa. Uncle Joey kept yelling, something about him not being cold, but I shut him out. I wanted to go over to Lisa. She looked so miserable. I shuffled my feet in the dust on the cave floor, thinking. If I did that, they'd maybe think I was for going back. Then that verse about loving each other came into my head. I shifted uneasily and walked over and put my hand on Lisa's arm. It was freezing and goose-bumpy, like raw chicken skin.

She looked up briefly and grabbed my hand, and suddenly I felt better. Uncle Joey abruptly stopped yelling. I looked up to find him staring at us.

Uncle Paul broke in, "Joey, you may not be cold, but Lisa has a smaller body mass and considerably less fat padding than you do. Being soaked can lead straight to hypothermia. It's dangerous."

"Right," Uncle Joey said softly, and sighed. "You're right. Anika goes over to Lisa to help. I'm her dad and all I can do is think of myself. Lisa is more important than any mountain."

There was a long silence. It made me feel odd to hear Uncle Joey talk like that. Lisa lifted her head and looked straight at her dad. I followed the direction of her gaze just in time to see him smile at her, really smile like he was seeing her as a person.

Then he looked toward Uncle Paul and said, "OK, what should we do, Paul?"

"Considering the rain, and our lack of gear—" Here he looked sharply at Uncle Joey. "I think going back would be the wisest—"

Mom interrupted. "Anika, did Rick go on up?"

I nodded, then added fiercely, "He never said he was Rick."

She wasn't listening. "If we get Lisa warm and it stops raining, will it be safe to continue?" she asked, looking at Uncle Paul.

He nodded slowly.

"Lisa, are you still willing to give it a go?" Uncle Joey asked in a gentler voice than I'd ever heard him use.

She looked up at him, bit her lip, and nodded.

"All right!" Traci yelled. "Then let's pray that the rain stops!"

We did that, holding hands in a circle.

Mom didn't pray about climbing at all. She said something about wanting the pattern of our lives to please God and bring him glory. Then she said, "You've promised to work all things together for good for those who love you and are called according to your purpose. Please work that out in our lives."

I peeked and watched her while other people prayed. I badly wanted to ask her what was happening. She didn't give me a chance.

"Who wants a cup of hot chocolate?" Mom asked as soon as we were done praying. She laughed when everybody yelled, "I do!" but it sounded like a fake laugh to me.

I watched her getting out a tiny stove. She looked so normal. I shook myself. Those things I'd been thinking couldn't be true. She was my mom. She and Daddy belonged together. Sandy and I were her only kids, and that was that.

"Silly," I said to myself. "Of course it's not true."

"What?" asked Lisa.

"Nothing," I answered quickly.

Lisa looked at me, frowning. Thank goodness Uncle Paul interrupted just then.

"Lisa, you and your dad better get into dry clothes."

Lisa's wet jeans were really stuck to her. She was so cold her hands wouldn't work properly.

"Are you sure you want to keep on?" I asked, tugging at her jeans leg.

"Uh-huh," she said between jerks. "Dad sounded like he really cares about me, for once."

"Come on, you guys, help," I called to Sandy and Traci, who were over by Mom. "I can't get these things off."

They came over and grabbed the other leg.

"Hey!" said Lisa, holding onto the rock she was sitting on. "Don't dump me in the dirt."

By the time we finally got Lisa dressed in dry clothes, the hot chocolate was ready. Mom passed around sandwiches and cookies. I sat there munching and staring at the rain. Drips came down so fast off the grass above the cave mouth that the cave had a silver bead curtain door.

My thoughts were going around and around. *Please let the rain stop. Let me at least try to make it. Please, please* . . . I would think. Then it would go the other way. I'd think, *But if we go up we might see that guy.* I shut that thought down in a hurry. I didn't want to ever see him again. But I did want to climb that mountain so much it hurt.

"Look!" Sandy said suddenly. "Look! It's stopping!"

The bead curtain was down to a few drips, and the slanting silver sheets of rain were gone. Everybody rushed to the cave mouth.

"Praise God!" bellowed Uncle Joey. "Come on, praise him with me." He started right in singing, "Praise God from whom all blessings flow . . ."

We all joined in. "Praise him, all creatures here below!"

A feeling of calm happiness washed over me. "Praise him above, ye heavenly hosts. Praise Father, Son, and Holy Ghost. Amen."

Just as we finished, the sun burst through a rip in the cloud. Everything glittered golden. The whole earth was praising him with us.

"All right!" I yelled, running out into the sunshine. My heel hurt, so I stopped and spun in a circle with my face to the sun. Traci and Sandy whooped and danced around too.

"God is still God no matter what, right?" I said to Lisa as I came back into the cave trying not to limp.

"You're crazy," she said, but she was grinning too.

A few minutes later we were packed and on our way.

"Ouch," I muttered under my breath in time to each step. "Ouch, ouch, ouch."

My heel burned, but I wasn't about to stop and look at it. Not now that we were on our way again.

Before long, we got to where the ground was dry and the grass clumps were smaller. We were walking up a long slope at an angle towards a ridge. This time I paid attention and stayed close to the others. We all trudged along at a slow, steady walk.

"Is that people?" Sandy stopped suddenly and pointed across the slope. She was right in front of me.

I tried to push past her. It was too hard to start again if you stopped.

"Uncle Paul!" she called. "Is that people?"

"OK, rest time," Uncle Paul called.

I flopped down and shut my eyes. My shoulders felt suddenly cool and light as the weight of the pack rested on a rock.

I could feel Uncle Paul's footsteps through the ground as he came up to us.

"What was that, Sandy?" His voice came out of the air above my head.

Sandy repeated her question for the third time. Then I heard Uncle Paul chuckle.

"Well?" she demanded.

"Anika," Uncle Paul said. I opened my eyes and squinted at him against the sun. "You wanted gnomes. Well, there they are."

I sat up and stared. There was something there. A group of upright shapes. I squinted to see better.

"Gnomes?" Sandy asked, staring hard at the things. "There is no such thing as gnomes," she added indignantly. "What's he talking about?"

"Gnome plants," I said, grinning. "Like in that book I saw. See, they're straight up and down like poles and covered with greenish gray hair."

"Everybody up!" Uncle Paul called. "We've got to keep moving to get to the Teleki Valley camp before dark."

"Uuuuugh!" groaned Uncle Joey. "You're a slave driver, Paul. I'm dying, and you force me onward."

He rolled onto his feet with another moan.

"Are you OK, Joey?" Mom asked. I think that was the first thing she'd said since we left the cave.

He laughed, but it wasn't a very loud laugh for Uncle Joey. "Except that I'm filthy, exhausted, and have a world-class headache, I'm fine. Paul, your high-altitude demons are getting to me."

"Demons?" Traci asked nervously, looking at her Dad.

That made Uncle Joey laugh. "Ow! Laughing hurts. Be careful, Traci, or they'll get you too. They suck the oxygen out of the air so your head aches. They make you dizzy and buzz your brain."

Lisa rolled her eyes at her dad, but she was smiling. Then she said, "It's not really demons, Traci. Your dad told us in the car that the Africans had never been in high altitude or really cold places. So when they started getting sick or frozen they thought evil spirits were attacking them."

"Are you sick?" Sandy demanded, looking at Uncle Joey.

"No," he said too loudly. "Let's move it."

My heel hurt worse every time we got up from a rest, but it would go numb after a bit. I just had to keep from limping for the first little ways. Lisa caught up to me, and we walked together.

"This place is weird," she said, motioning around.

I nodded, too out of breath to say much. It was weird and beautiful. Silver-brown grass stretched down across the folds of the mountain. Here and there were clumps of gnome plants looking like old men at a committee meeting. There were also big cabbage-y plants. Some were low down, like giant green chrysanthemum flowers on the ground. Others were up on poles, like very strange baggy palm trees. I felt light, and hollow, and odd with space and wild sky around me.

Everything seemed strange, like one of those dreams you have when you're half asleep. My head ached. My thoughts felt pulled out of shape like Silly Putty. Worry about Mom and "Rick" twisted together and spread thin over the awesome weird beauty of the mountain.

Lisa didn't talk anymore either. I could hear her breathing hard. Even though she was just behind me, I felt alone. My body fell into a rhythm of walking. After a bit we came over a ridge.

"We're in Teleki Valley. It will be easier going now." Uncle Paul's voice sounded far away. My ears were buzzing. "Take a break. I'll keep moving and get supper started."

It suddenly seemed harder to stop than to keep going. I didn't want my shoulders and heel to get unnumb. Walking seemed automatic. Everybody else sat down. I kept walking behind Uncle Paul. He looked back at me, nodded once, and kept going.

The path got less steep. I seemed to float along. The aching weight of my pack was like a hand on my back pushing me. In my dizzy head the mountain seemed alive. The rough, tawny grass was fur, and I walked along a wide, soft fold in its hide. The path jogged around a boulder, and I looked down Teleki Valley to the real world. It was far away, far down from where the mountain held me up. Way down there, a lake shone silver like a dropped sequin.

I looked up. Sun struck my eyes, making me squint. It was hard to see clearly against the sun. The peaks were clear of cloud. They were huge and seemed as high as the moon. For a few seconds it seemed perfectly logical. The Kikuyu were right. This live mountain, huger than the world, was where God lived.

It gradually soaked into my dizzy head. God, the real God, my God, is bigger than that. Bigger than this whole mountain. Bigger than the universe.

"I ask the Father in his great glory to give you the power to be strong" went through my head from those verses I'd been reading. *Father in his great glory!* echoed in my head. The bigness of God filled me up until I thought I would explode with the wonder of it. Mount Kenya was another creature of his, like me, like animals. I felt held down to the mountain by the weight of my pack, small on the mountain in front of him.

"Strength out of his great glory"? I thought and tried to figure it out. Strength enough for anything, for mountains. *Does it fit with this Rick thing somehow?* I wondered, but I couldn't concentrate, and the thought slid away. I was walking in a dizzy daze.

The sun went behind the mountain's shoulder. We

walked in shadow. Nelion and Mbatian still stood in the sun, high in a burnished sky. We walked on and on.

My body was on automatic. The complaints of my heel, shoulders, and even my aching head seemed far away. When Uncle Paul finally stopped, I walked straight into his back. The hard canvas of his pack smacked my face. I stumbled and sat down.

He looked at me and chuckled. "Sleeping on the march? Come on, we're just about there."

His hand felt warm and rough as he hauled me to my feet. "Take a drink at the creek," he said, kneeling and scooping up water.

I hadn't noticed that we were right on the edge of a noisy brook. I looked at him blankly, trying to connect.

He looked up with water running off his beard. "Come on, drink up."

I shook my head to clear it and got down to drink. My pack just about pitched me into the water head-first. I stuck out my hands to catch my balance. They hit the water with a splash that soaked my face. Luckily the water was only about three inches deep. I gasped and woke up properly. My ears popped and quit buzzing.

Suddenly everything hurt. Also I'd never felt so tired in my life. I looked around. We were in the bottom of the valley. About the length of a football field away, there was a hut and a bunch of tents.

Uncle Paul chuckled again. I must have looked really out of it. Then he stood up and started across the stream. I tried to get up. Ow! My shoulders felt like they were coming off.

I tried again and this time made it to my feet. I splashed across the creek, not even bothering about stepping-stones, and followed Uncle Paul. *Just a few more steps. Just a little way,* I thought, staring at the back of Uncle Paul's legs. I didn't even try not to limp. Uncle Paul's boots walked steadily across the grass and into the hut.

It was almost completely dark inside. Uncle Paul was busy doing something with his pack. The only thing I paid any attention to was a wooden shelf across the hut. There was room for seven or eight sleeping bags. I shrugged my shoulders and shoved my pack straps off. My pack hit the floor with a thud, and I hit the shelf bed facedown. I lay there thinking, *I'll get up in a minute. I'll get up and help Uncle Paul.*

Chapter
Seven

~~~~~~

"No, none for me!" Uncle Joey's voice boomed. I jumped
and struggled to sit up. The side of my face was gooey
from sleeping facedown on the hard shelf. I wiped at it
with the back of my hand and tried to figure out where
I was.

Uncle Joey's voice went on, "Better leave my mis-
treated stomach empty if I want to climb tomorrow."

I looked wildly around, trying to see in the pitch
dark. A blanket or something was tangled around me.
My cheekbone hurt from the hard boards. I rubbed it
and tried to think. *Climb? Oh, Mount Kenya, at the
hut.*

The smell of food made my mouth water. I shoved
aside the thing tangling up my legs and stood up.
"Ouch!" I gasped and grabbed my left foot. Wow, did
that heel ever hurt now! Still I wasn't going to miss supper. I got to my feet and felt for the door. Something
tripped me, and I bumped the door and staggered out
into the light.

"The sleeper awakes!" Uncle Joey boomed.

"Your hair is sticking straight up," Sandy said, bursting into giggles.

I blinked at her, trying to get my head together. Everybody was sitting in a circle around a fire and a pot of food. There was a lamp lit.

Mom came towards me and smoothed my hair. "You OK, Anika? You looked so peaceful I didn't want to wake you. I covered you with your sleeping bag."

"Um, Mom," I interrupted. "Is there an outhouse or something here?"

"I'll show you, but put this on."

She handed me my jacket, and I shrugged into its thick canvas warmth. The movement made my shoulders ache again. I followed her, limping across the frosty grass. It looked silver in the moonlight.

When I came out, Mom had her back to me and was looking up at the peaks. They stood huge and black in the bright silver light.

"I will lift up mine eyes to the hills, from whence cometh my help," Mom said, then she added in a more determined voice, "My help cometh from the Lord, which made heaven and earth."

It was the psalm Daddy had read, only King James Version. I hung back, wondering if she was thinking about God helping her with this Rick thing.

She turned and put her arm around me. "We have a great God, don't we?"

I nodded, not sure what to say. Instead I looked at the peaks high in the huge silver-lit sky. The mountain's beauty and power swelled over me until no room was left. I stood still, drinking it in.

"Anika, there's something I need to tell you," Mom said.

I froze, dreading what she would say.

"I should have told you before, but I wanted to do this climb so much first." She sighed, and I squirmed. "When I was a teenager I did something very foolish. . . ." There was a long pause. "I . . . um . . . got involved with a boy in a way I shouldn't have, and—"

Suddenly I was angry. She was supposed to say it wasn't true. Rick *was not* her kid! I didn't want to hear it.

"Mom, can't we just go back? I'm starving," I blurted.

I twisted away from her and hurried toward the others. She came after me and caught my shoulder. I flinched and twisted away again.

"Anika, you're limping badly."

"My heel hurts," I said, glad to get her attention away from the thing I didn't even want to think about. It was like a monster just outside the door. If I didn't open the door and look at it, maybe it would go away. A sore foot was easier to deal with.

"I want to take a look at that in the light."

I nodded, but I still kept hurrying to get away from her.

"Hungry, Anika?" Uncle Paul asked, handing me a bowl of steaming stew.

The hot, meaty stew was the best thing I ever ate. It warmed up my cold, hungry body.

"At least somebody is getting some good out of Elsie's stew," Uncle Joey said. "I figured a good hot meal would be worth the extra weight to pack it in. But it didn't do me much good."

"Why not?" I asked, surprised.

"I don't think my stomach is too keen on food right now."

"Speaking of stomachaches and such, who is planning to go on tomorrow?" Uncle Paul asked. "The ones who aren't able can sleep in and wait for the rest of us here."

"I'm going!" I blurted through a mouthful of stew.

"Anika, I want to check your foot out first," Mom said.

"But Mom! It gets numb after I walk a bit. I'm going!" I insisted. "You're wrecking my life!"

Mom looked like I had slapped her in the face. There was a dead silence and everybody stared at me. I ducked my head, frowning furiously. Mom *was* wrecking everything. First Rick, and then not letting me climb.

After a second Uncle Paul kept on with finding out who was going. I listened but I wouldn't look up at Mom.

"Lisa?" he asked. "You were looking pretty miserable earlier."

"I'm OK now. I want to try," she said.

"Good for you, Lisa, that's the spirit," Uncle Joey said almost as loud as usual. "I'll give it a try too, Paul. After all I can't let my little girl beat me."

"Hazel?" Uncle Paul asked.

"I feel fine, but I want to check Anika's foot. I'll stay back with her."

"Mom, I'm going!" I insisted.

"Not if you don't let me look at that foot," she said in the voice that means it's no use arguing.

I had to grit my teeth hard to keep from yelling when she pulled my boot off. My stomach felt sick when I looked. The whole heel of my sock was red.

"Anika!" Mom said, sounding shocked. "You tould have shold me!"

"Huh?" said Uncle Joey.

She peeled off my sock. There was a raw spot about as big as a quarter. The cold air made it sting. For a second I wanted to stay back. I clenched my teeth. It would be really stupid to get this far and stop.

"It's just a rubbed-off blister," I insisted. "Really, it gets numb after a bit when I walk."

85

"You sure you want to try?" Mom asked gently.

I nodded without looking at her.

"You're going to have to walk on it anyway. If we get it clean and covered with moleskin, you can give it a try. Sandy, would you get the first-aid kit out of my pack? Then I want all you kids to check your feet for blisters. If Anika had done something about this when it started, we wouldn't have this mess."

It turned out that everybody checked their feet, even the grown-ups. Uncle Paul said to wash them good and get clean socks on. I'd never thought about it, but he said keeping your feet healthy is one of the most important things when you're out in the wilderness. A couple of other people had blisters, but not like mine.

"It's going to hurt worse tomorrow," Mom said.

I grunted and turned my back on her to pull on my socks.

Lisa came and sat by me. "What's the matter, Anika?" she whispered.

I muttered, "Nothing" without looking up at her.

"So you don't have to be so stuck-up," she said, sounding upset.

"So maybe I'm afraid I won't make it up the mountain tomorrow," I said, trying to head her off. The only trouble was, saying it made me realize how true it was. On top of everything else I really was scared I wouldn't make it. My heel hurt a lot. Also I'd had a headache all afternoon, and maybe that meant I was starting to get altitude-sick.

"Oh," she said, "you will. You were first here, weren't you?"

"That doesn't count. I was really out of it," I said, carefully pulling my sock over the bandage on my heel.

"It's me that won't make it. I want to because of Dad."

She sounded so sad that I looked up at her. "At least you don't have a bad foot," I said.

"I just want Dad to think I'm OK for once." She paused, then added, "I asked God, so maybe it will be OK."

"Yeah, maybe it will be OK," I said softly, not just thinking about the mountain.

"Hey, I know," Lisa said. "Let's—"

"Anika! Lisa!" Mom called. "Come on, you two. Bed-time. Hurry up."

"But, Mom, I don't have my boot back on," I said.

"Hop then. You've got to take it off for bed anyway. Sandy and Traci are already tucked in. We've all got to get to bed early so we'll be ready to get up before dawn."

"Before dawn?" Lisa squeaked, stopping halfway to the hut.

I laughed and hopped after her.

"I don't do 'before dawn,'" she insisted.

"So you're staying back?" I asked, grabbing her shoulder to keep my balance.

"No way. But they're not going anywhere." She flapped her hand at the peaks showing in the moonlight. "I don't see why we have to get up so early."

"Don't ask me. People who climb just do," I said, hopping toward the door.

It was cold getting changed. We decided to put on the inside layer of the clothes we were going to wear the next day. I snuggled into my sleeping bag, hugging myself against the cold. Uncle Joey came in to read us the Bible.

He stood there in the flickering light of the lantern and read, "'But the people who trust the Lord will become strong again. They will be able to rise up as an eagle in the sky. They will run without needing rest. They will walk without becoming tired.'"

"Does that mean we can get to the top for sure if we just trust God, or whatever?" Traci asked.

Uncle Paul chuckled, but didn't say anything. He was leaning against the wall, and the dim light made his beard look even bigger.

"Well?" Traci demanded.

"No, I guess not," said Uncle Joey after a bit. "Actually, that's why I read it, to encourage myself. But you're right. It doesn't exactly fit. I think it means God will give us the strength to do the things we need to do,

88

the things that are right. I guess making it to the top of Mount Kenya isn't exactly essential."

"It is to me!" Sandy said, and everybody laughed.

Uncle Joey asked Mom to pray. In her prayer she thanked God for the reminder that his strength was enough for any situation. I didn't get the feeling she was talking about the mountain.

The adults went out to the fire just outside the door. I could hear their voices coming softly through the wall as I waited for my sleeping bag to warm up. After a minute I realized that I could feel my heart beating like I was running. I was breathing hard too.

"I think I'm dying," Traci whispered suddenly.

Sandy sat up straight in her sleeping bag and yelled, "Mom!"

"What is it?" Uncle Joey asked, opening the door.

"Traci's dying!" Sandy blurted.

Traci sat up and said, "My heart is going too fast."

Uncle Joey bellowed with laughter. "So's mine, and I'd bet my bottom dollar so is every one of the other kids'. It's the high-altitude demons again."

"What d'you mean?" Traci asked, sounding irritated.

"Look at it this way," he explained. "The air is too thin, so you have to breathe more to get enough oxygen, and your heart has to pump more to take enough oxygen to your body."

"Oh," she said, and lay down.

"Sleep tight, kids," Uncle Joey said, and he shut the door, still chuckling.

After a bit Traci said, "It feels weird, trying to go to sleep breathing like you're running."

"Shhh!" Lisa and I both hissed.

I half woke up when the adults came to bed. They shoved everybody over, and Lisa ended up partly on top of me. I didn't care because that was warmer. Somebody was snoring. I pulled my sleeping bag over my face to get out of the cold. Traci jabbed me hard with her knee. I shoved her off.

Whanggg! Bang! The noise echoed in my head. I tried to sit up and couldn't. People were yelling. I thrashed and finally found the top of the sleeping bag and got my face out. I gasped for breath and sat up. A flashlight beam was dancing around the hut.

"What happened?" Lisa asked sleepily.

"Your dad knocked the pot and kettle down," Sandy said.

"There was something in here! There was!" Uncle Joey insisted. "Some animal, and I reached for the flashlight and hit the pots first."

"Well, I think you got rid of it pretty efficiently," Mom said, half laughing.

Uncle Paul's sleeping bag turned over with a thump,

and he said something like, "Just hyraxes . . . hyraxes . . . sleep." It thumped over again and held still.

"Hyraxes?" Uncle Joey asked. "Oh, those rabbity things that are supposed to be related to elephants. I thought they lived in trees."

I sighed and lay down again. All that noise for a dumb hyrax.

Mom laughed, "Tree hyraxes do."

"Rock hyraxes!" Uncle Paul's sleeping bag said loudly. "Saw them yesterday . . . beg food all over the camp. Must be blind. Sleep!"

"OK, OK, I get the point," Uncle Joey said, and he lay back down.

It seemed like I'd only been asleep about ten minutes when somebody's watch alarm went off. The high, piercing beep kept on and on. I dragged my eyes open. It was pitch dark.

Something thumped over on the end where Uncle Paul was, and the beep quit.

"Dawn in a hour," he grunted. There were more thumps. There was a gust of cold air, and the door banged shut behind Uncle Paul.

This is it; this is the day, I thought, and I sat up with a jerk. It felt like I'd knocked my brain loose, because my head started aching like fury. Also I had to go to the bathroom.

So what, I thought and grinned. *This is the day I get to the top of Lenana peak of Mount Kenya.* I leaned on one elbow and felt for my clothes along the wall where I'd left them.

"Ow!" Lisa complained in a muffled voice. "Get your elbow off me."

I jerked back.

"Stop it, Anika!" Traci snapped from the other side of me. "Get off me."

"Sorrreee!" I said, stuffing a sweatshirt over the T-shirt I'd slept in. I pulled off the sleeping bag and fumbled to get my jeans on over my sweatpants. *Brrr!* It was cold.

My feet bumped my boots as I climbed off the shelf. I felt around to turn them right side up and stuffed them on. Wow, did that hurt my heel! I gritted my teeth and limped out the door, heading for the outhouse.

As soon as I was outside I wished I'd stopped to put on my jacket. I hugged myself and limped faster. The moon was behind the edge of the mountain, but you could still see—sort of, anyway. The grass was pale silver and crunchy with frost.

When I came out of the outhouse, I stood still, shivering, and looked up at the peaks. They rose up, high and black, into the dim silver sky. There was a wide light streak above the mountain shoulder from where the moon was. I guess you could call it a moonset. Straight overhead, away from the moonlight, the stars looked close enough to touch.

I shivered again harder, partly because I was excited, then, forgetting all about my heel, I ran for the hut.

When I stopped by the door, I almost fell. Whew, was I dizzy, and my head was banging in time to my heart-beat. I leaned my head against the cold door to catch my balance. My stomach heaved up and down like a bird's nest at the end of a branch in a high wind.

"Stupid," I muttered between gasps for breath, "stupid, stupid, you don't run at fourteen thousand feet." I wasn't going in until I could look normal.

Gradually my head stopped spinning. Suddenly the door opened, pulling away from my head. I lost my balance and staggered forward, running straight into Lisa.

"Sorry," I blurted, trying to catch my balance.

"You OK?" she asked.

"I'm fine!" I said it so loud that everybody turned to look at me. My head was still thumping so hard it made me want to shut my eyes. I sat down on the shelf and started stuffing my sleeping bag. After a few seconds, people looked away. I leaned my head on the top of my pack, hoping no one would notice I wasn't doing anything. After a bit, my head quit hurting so much.

"Is Uncle Joey OK?" Sandy asked, walking in the door.

"Why?" asked Uncle Paul, who was stuffing his sleeping bag into his pack.

"Well, he was ahead of me coming back. All of a sudden he just sat down on a rock and put his head in his hands. He didn't answer when I asked if he was OK either."

Uncle Paul just grunted and stuck his jacket on.

"Well?" Sandy demanded, but Uncle Paul had left.

"Traci! Traci!" Sandy said, shaking her friend's sleeping bag. "Get up! It's time to climb."

Just then Mom came in, letting a burst of cold air into the stuffy, crowded, messy little room. If she saw how I felt, she'd keep me back for sure.

Chapter
Eight

~~~~~~~~~~

"Anika, since you're dressed, could you go get some
water for breakfast?" Mom asked. "Take the big pot Joey
knocked over."

The cold air made me realize I'd forgotten my jacket
again, but I wasn't going back now. The sky was pale
gray in the east now. I took a deep breath of cold air,
and my head felt better. I looked up at the peaks again,
then stopped and faced them. The verse echoed in my
head, *"The Father in his great glory."*

"I ask the Father in his great glory to give me
strength," I whispered, and shivered. "Please help me to
make it," I prayed. "Help me not to get dizzy again."

I didn't mention the whole thing about Mom and
Rick. It seemed like a worse mountain than the real
one, and I didn't even want to think about it. A violent
shiver reminded me that I'd better get the water and get
back inside. Somebody passed me a little ways over. It
looked like that Rick guy again. I kept my eyes down
and veered out of his way.

The water was biting cold on my hands where I splashed myself filling the pot.

After breakfast I pulled my Bible out. I wanted to read the part again about how God would give me strength.

The funny thing was, when I read that part, it seemed like the whole thing was about love instead of strength. Verse 17 said, "I pray that your life will be strong in love and be built on love."

Does that mean I have to make things OK with Mom? How can I, if— I swallowed. Maybe nothing was really wrong anyway. Nobody had actually *said* that Rick was Mom's kid. Maybe it was all my imagination. I shivered and looked down at the next part to get away from what I was thinking.

It said, "I pray that you and all God's holy people will have the power to understand the greatness of Christ's love. I pray that you can understand how wide and how long and how high and how deep that love is."

"Come on, Anika, let's move it!" Uncle Paul called, coming out of the hut.

We locked our stuff in the hut and didn't carry anything but water. Mom walked with Sandy and Traci, so I stayed in front with Uncle Paul. I didn't want to face her. The sun wasn't up properly. The light was a clear pale gray, but there was a gold in the east. We walked up the valley, then the path turned and zigzagged up the scree.

Scree is sharp little rocks. It's all the bits that have broken off the higher peaks, like a giant gravel heap dumped down the side of the mountain. Soon I was stopping after every four steps to catch my breath. The icy rocks crunched under my boots.

Crunch, crunch, crunch, crunch, pause and pant four times, then *crunch, crunch, crunch, crunch.*

My head was hurting again. I wasn't first in line anymore. Both Lisa and Sandy were ahead of me now. My hands, face, and feet hurt from the cold.

There was a shuffle, a clatter of gravel, then a tremendous sound almost like a roar. *"OUAGGH!"*

I spun around. Uncle Joey was off the path throwing up.

"Gross!" I heard Sandy say. Uncle Joey barfed again, and Sandy said, "Lisa, your dad must be the world's loudest puker."

Lisa didn't answer. Uncle Joey finished and walked up the path toward us. He flapped his hands, motioning for us to keep walking. Lisa went back and walked with him.

A little later he threw up again. We kept going. I bunched my cold hands into a fist in the middle of my mittens. That was a bit better, but they still hurt. I wondered if when your hands hurt from cold it meant you were getting frostbite. Mostly I didn't think anything at all.

A little later Mom's voice stopped us. "Paul, your daughter wants you."

I took a quick look back and then flopped down flat to rest. We were going to be here for long enough to rest anyway. I'd seen Traci sitting on the ground, huddled in a lump, crying. Uncle Paul's boots crunched back past me.

I could hear Uncle Paul's soft, low voice, then Traci's voice rose in a high wail: "I want to go *home!* I feel sick, and my feet are cold. They *hurt!*" She started howling like a baby.

"Someone will have to go back with her," Mom said.

There was a long pause. I thought Uncle Joey would go back because he was sick. He didn't say anything. Finally Uncle Paul said, "Would you be confident of the path if I went back?"

There was another pause. After a bit, Mom said, "I'll take her back."

I sat up. That wasn't fair! Without thinking, I was totally on Mom's side. She wasn't sick like Uncle Joey, and Traci wasn't even her kid. Mom wanted to climb so much. Then I remembered about Rick, and she seemed like a stranger. I turned my head away.

Sandy went back with Mom and Traci. She said she felt sick too, but I think she just didn't want to keep going without her friend and Mom.

Lisa, Uncle Paul, Uncle Joey, and I kept walking. Sunlight was on the peaks now, and it washed down towards us like a slow, gold ocean. My head hurt. My lungs hurt. I wanted to stop walking and lie there. Instead we kept on making slow steps up the scree. Every tiny detail seemed bigger than life, like a close-up in a movie.

I saw why the gravel made such loud crunching noises. A lot of the little pieces of stone were up on tiny ice towers. Each step smashed the tiny towers. Before long, sunlight washed over us.

"OK, rest time," Uncle Paul finally said.

I flopped flat onto my back and lay there with my eyes shut against the sun. My chest heaved. After a bit, my breathing slowed down. I could hear Uncle Joey breathing hard, rattling, gasping breaths. I didn't move or open my eyes. It felt so good to hold still. After a bit I noticed soft, musical tinkling noises all around us.

Something made a noise like a tiny chime right by my ear. I turned my head sideways and squinted against the light. There was nothing but gravel and ice glinting in the sun.

Ching! This time I saw it. One of the tiny ice pedestals had broken and fallen down making a noise like a tiny bell. I sat up. All around us, the sun was warming the scree, playing a soft, bright tune on the breaking ice pedestals.

"Listen," I blurted. "The sun and the mountain are singing together!"

Uncle Paul gave me a funny look.

"They are!" I insisted.

Uncle Joey grumbled and sat up, "Whether they are or not, they'll just have to do it without me. I have to quit. I thought maybe I'd feel better after a bit, but it just keeps getting worse. I should have gone back with the kids. Hazel could be here but for my stupid pride."

My mouth dropped open.

"Anybody coming with me?" he asked.

There was a long silence. Finally Uncle Joey heaved himself to his feet, said, "See you down there," and started down.

He'd gone about ten steps when Lisa suddenly said, "Wait! Wait, Dad, I'll come with you," and took off after him. He stopped and reached out his hand. She took it and they started down together.

I watched them for a minute. Things were looking good between Lisa and her dad, anyway, but how about me? I looked anxiously at Uncle Paul. He raised one bushy red eyebrow then looked up the mountain, silently asking me a question.

"Can we?" I blurted. "Can we keep on?"

"I don't know if we can," he said, grinning, "but we may try. You ready to go on?"

I nodded and stood up. When I looked up the long, sun-swept slope of scree my heart sank. It was too high, too far. I swallowed and reminded myself, *The Father in his great glory will give me strength*.

We didn't talk. There was no breath left for talk. My stomach felt like lead. Once it got so bad I thought I was going to throw up. I sat down and held my head in my hands. After a second I felt better. When I looked up, Uncle Paul was waiting for me.

I swallowed hard and whispered between breaths, "If I make it, it's all you, God."

I stood up and we kept on, taking steps and resting, taking steps and resting. When we rested I could see far, far down. The tents and cabins in the camp where we slept in Teleki Valley looked smaller than pieces of rice. Mostly we couldn't see the peaks, only the next ridge above us.

This time the thing that kept going through my head in time to my breathing was *strong . . . in . . . love . . . strong . . . in . . . love.* I didn't think about what it meant.

After a long time the scree leveled out. We were walking through round, black boulders. I wasn't watching where we were going, only looking at the back of Uncle Paul's pack. Suddenly he went through a door.

I stopped and stood swaying, thinking, *A door? Here?*

It was a little wooden cabin. Inside I flopped onto the floor, too tired to ask what a cabin was doing here. After a bit I heard Uncle Paul chuckle, and I sat up.

He was looking at a big leather book.

"What is it?" I asked. "What is this place?"

He grinned at me through his beard. "It's top hut. Where the real climbers stay before they tackle Nelion or Mbatian. This is a visitors book. You can sign it. Some of the entries are great. Look at this one from Australia."

I got up, caught my balance, and went over. But when I looked at it, I froze. It wasn't what the guys from Australia wrote, it was the last thing written that got me.

It said, "Rick, climbing this mother of a mountain looking for my mother." My mouth got dry, and I stood still, staring into space. That guy *was* Rick. And he'd said, "looking for my mother." I felt sick.

"Here, sign it, you've earned it," Uncle Paul said, holding out a pen.

I jumped and shook my head and stumbled out the door. After a minute Uncle Paul came out and we started off. He never asked why I'd run out of the cabin. For once I was glad he wasn't a talker.

It wasn't so steep now. We were very high up. That

high place didn't seem like part of planet Earth. Once someone told me that on the Himalayas you can see stars in the daytime because you're so far up through the earth's atmosphere. I didn't see any stars, but the sky was darker blue than it should have been. There was only ice, barren black rock, and empty space.

Then we came into the snow. At first it was just patches in the shadows of the rocks. Then it was a thin layer. For a while each step Uncle Paul took left a perfect mold of the bottom of his boot.

"This is going to be tough," Uncle Paul said as we stopped to rest. He was panting hard, and there were icicles on his beard.

How can it get worse? I wondered, frantically gasping for breath. After a bit, Uncle Paul said, "Ready to go?"

I jerked my head yes and got up.

The next part was like a bad dream. Endless stumbling after Uncle Paul's boots . . . the snow getting deeper . . . getting harder and harder to walk . . . no thinking, no looking around, nothing except keeping going. Time stopped. The sun went away. I'd been climbing, stumbling, struggling in snow behind Uncle Paul's boots forever. Torn bits of mist blew by.

"Almost there," Uncle Paul panted. "Anika, look up."

I squinted and looked, swaying on my feet. The slope swelled steeply upward, then black rocks poked through. There was nothing above the rocks but mist. The top of Lenana!

I stood, taking huge gasps for air. That last steep snow slope seemed impossible.

"Please, God. Please, God," I wheezed as I breathed in and out. Each time Uncle Paul stopped I was a little farther behind. I wanted to quit. Just to say, "I can't— I'm stopping," and rest.

I fell flat on my face and lay there. Cold snow bit my cheeks. Warm tears trickled through the cold. *How can I get this far and not make it?!*

I could hear boots crunching toward me through the snow. I figured it was Uncle Paul and turned my head away. I didn't want him to know I was crying. The boots stopped beside me.

"Hey kid, you OK?"

I gasped and spun around, stumbling to my feet. It was that Rick guy! He was looking straight at me. I ducked my head and wiped at my runny nose.

"Hey, it's not that bad," he said. He waved his arms with a huge grin on his face. "I beat this mountain."

He shook his fist and threw his head back, and yelled, "I *beat* you! Do you *hear me?*" His voice echoed triumphantly off the far peaks. Suddenly he quit and looked back at me. "I'm ready for anything now. Where's your mom?"

After the yelling I wasn't ready for that. Without thinking, I blurted, "She went back with Sandy."

"To the Teleki Valley camp?" he asked, but I just glared at him. *How could I have told him,* I wondered. *He has nothing to do with us!*

He grinned and thumped me on the shoulder. "Don't worry, you'll make it, Sis. I did."

He spun away from me and started down. I staggered from the thump and yelled after him, "No! It's not true!"

He stopped and looked up, grinning. "OK, so you won't make it," and strode off through the snow.

"That's not what I meant," I muttered furiously. I'd show him! "I . . . will . . . I . . . will . . . show . . . him!" I muttered between breaths, stomping determinedly through the snow up the last slope.

"Who?" asked a voice right beside me. I jumped. I'd almost run into Uncle Paul.

"Nobody!" I answered, ducking away from him.

"Like the nobody you were just talking to?" he asked between panting breaths.

I didn't answer. Two could play at being quiet. Besides, I didn't have enough breath for talking. I needed it all for climbing. I stomped past Uncle Paul.

"Sure put a fire under you," Uncle Paul said, chuckling, as he caught up. "I thought you were going to quit for a minute back there."

"I . . . have . . . to . . . make . . . it," I gasped between breaths with my teeth clenched.

"Good," he said, behind me.

It was quiet except for our rasping breath and the noise of our boots in the snow. A few feet later I wasn't sure I could keep going. It was too hard.

"I . . . have . . . to," I gasped in a whisper in time to my steps. My throat hurt from breathing so hard.

"Rest!" Uncle Paul said, putting his hand on my shoulder. I collapsed into the snow and gasped for breath.

It's no use, I thought.

Uncle Paul got to his feet. "Let's move," he said.

I didn't budge. It *was* too hard. My gasping breaths were almost sobs. It just wasn't fair—the mountain, this Rick person. Nothing was fair.

Uncle Paul stood looking down at me. Then he said something that really shocked me.

"I guess he was right. He said you're a quitter."

"He didn't say that!" I half yelled. "And I am not!"

"So show me," Uncle Paul said in a way that sounded like he was making fun of me.

I glared at him and dragged myself to my feet. The snow was a monster holding my feet down. I fought that beautiful white monster, grimly putting one foot in front of the other. My lungs hurt. The monster got stronger and stronger. I stumbled and fell on my face.

"Anika! Anika!" Uncle Paul said between harsh breaths. I ignored him. A big hand shook my shoulder. "Anika, look up!"

I dragged myself into a sitting position and looked. We were only about ten yards from the top! This time I didn't even bother to get up. I crawled that last ten yards.

Uncle Paul reached out a hand to me for the last bit, but I ignored it. I clambered up the black boulder on the top and flopped onto my back. The only thing above me was sky. I'd made it! Happiness flooded me, right from my toes to my ears. I lay there gasping for breath and grinning.

Chapter
Nine

So what if the sky I was looking at was gray. So what
about anything! I'd made it. Flat on my back, I
stretched my arms out and laughed.

Uncle Paul chuckled and said, "God sent that charac-
ter along at the right time."

I twisted to look at Uncle Paul. How could he know
anything about Rick? Uncle Paul was grinning through
a screen of icicles hanging off his mustache. I sighed
with relief. He didn't really know, or he wouldn't be
grinning like that.

"You were just about finished," Uncle Paul said. "I
don't know what that kid said, but it got you moving
again."

"Oh." I felt like someone had dumped my thoughts
upside down. This whole thing with Rick wasn't just a
trick God played to get me up the mountain, was it? Suddenly I knew a trick that Uncle Paul had played, though.

"You called me a quitter to make me keep going!" I
blurted.

He chuckled again and said, "I never called you a quitter."

I frowned, trying to remember. Looking at things the other way around made me dizzy. Could things I hated really be on my side, helping me? Finally I said, "God sure answers prayers funny ways."

Uncle Paul laughed right out loud, then said, "Don't you think we ought to thank him?"

I nodded doubtfully, then grinned. Uncle Paul was right. God had helped me get up the mountain. All the ways he'd done it suddenly clicked into place. Letting me get a jacket, helping me find the path when I'd gotten lost. He'd used other people, like Lisa getting me a chance to come, Mom finding all the stuff, Uncle Paul keeping going with me and making me keep going, and even me being mad about Rick. Suddenly bowing my head and praying quietly wasn't enough.

I leapt to my feet, stretched out my arms, and yelled, "Thanks, God! Thaaa-ank youuuu Go-od!!"

My shout disappeared into the wide space like it had been swallowed. Cool, snowy air out of the vast space around me pressed against my cheeks. *I'm on top of Lenana Peak!* I thought. I was smiling so wide that my cheeks ached.

Uncle Paul's big laugh brought me back down to

earth. "Amen!" he said, still chuckling. A swirl of snow wrapped around us.

"We'd better get down off here before we can't see where we're going."

I turned back for one more look as we started down.

"Come on, Anika, move it. We've got to get out of this snow," Uncle Paul called. "Let's go tell your mom you made it all the way. Besides, we need to get started so we can make it back to the lodge before dark tonight."

The thought of Mom made me frown for a second, but not for long. In fact, before we'd gone very far I had myself almost convinced that the whole thing with Rick would turn out to be a big mistake—that it was all just something God did to help me get up the mountain. I couldn't stop grinning. I'd actually made it to the top of Lenana Peak.

"All right!" I yelled, watching Uncle Paul. We were back down at the top of the scree. It was still cloudy out, but the snow had stopped. Without saying a word he'd looked back at me, grinning, then taken a huge leap into space. He hit the scree about thirty feet down the steep hill, spraying gravel in all directions. He skidded to a stop, then turned and waved his arm at me to come on.

That's when I yelled. It looked like *fun!* I took two running steps and leaped. *Wheee!* I sailed way downhill over the scree and then hit, skidding on my behind, in a little avalanche of gravel. It was fun!

I hadn't gone as far as Uncle Paul. He looked up at me, grinning through his red beard.

"Just make sure you land so you don't fall forward onto your face," he called, then he leaped again.

I scrambled to my feet and followed. He waited, but it took me two more jumps to catch up because his jumps were so much longer.

"This is great!" I said, laughing. "I thought scree was almost the worst, but it's the best part coming down."

The distance seemed a lot shorter coming down than going up. Before long we were walking through the tough clumps of grass above camp.

"Anika! Anika! Did you make it?"

It was Lisa, coming up the path to us. I laughed and ran toward her. She grabbed my arm and swung me around.

"Well?" she asked, grinning.

"Yes!" I yelled. *"Yes!* God helped me make it all the way!"

"Way to go!" she yelled, and we spun around, laughing. "Come on, they're waiting for you with lunch."

"Good, I'm starved," Uncle Paul said right behind us. We started walking again, and he asked, "Lisa, how's your dad?"

"Oh, he's OK now. He's still got a headache, but he said it isn't as bad as it was." She paused and turned to face me. "Anika, there's this guy—you know—the one that kept bugging us. Well, he's with your mom. He came, and she left with him. It was really weird."

I stopped dead, feeling like I was choking. Then I shook my head. I was fed up with being scared and worried.

"Where are they?" I demanded. I was going to clear this up once and for all. Besides, I wanted to tell Mom I'd made it to the top.

Lisa pointed. Three people were walking down by the creek. *Sandy's with them!* I thought, and I headed off at a trot towards them.

"What's going on?" Lisa yelled after me.

I shrugged and kept going. Usually I would have yelled to Mom and Sandy that I'd made it, but suddenly I was scared. What was Rick doing with them? I dropped to a walk.

Mom looked up and saw me coming just before I got to them, and she gave me a big smile.

"Anika! You're back!"

"Did you make it all the way?" Sandy blurted. "Rick said you were almost there."

Rick said! I thought, and I looked at him uneasily. He was smiling and standing very close to Mom. I ducked my head away from him.

"Well?" Mom asked.

"I did, right to the top!" Saying that made me feel better. I *had* made it!

Mom grabbed me and hugged me. "Congratulations, my gig birl." I laughed and hugged her back for a second, then pulled away.

Sandy was jumping up and down, saying, "You did it! You did it!"

Rick thumped me on the arm. "I knew you could do it, Sis!"

"I am *not* your sister," I yelled.

There was a dead silence. Rick looked like I'd hit him.

"Yes," Sandy whispered. "Mom said."

"No!" I yelled. "It's a mistake!"

"Anika," Mom said in a quiet voice. "Rick is your half brother. I was trying to tell you last night."

"How do you know it's him?" I said, spinning to glare at Rick again. He and Sandy were next to each other. They both had exactly the same blank, upset look on their face. Their eyes were even the same color.

I turned and ran. I just went straight ahead, not thinking about where I was going. I wanted out of there. In a minute I was stumbling and gasping with tiredness and lack of air. I dropped to a walk, but kept going.

"Aniiika! Aniiika! Stop!" I could hear Mom yelling. Sandy was yelling at me to stop too.

"No," I whispered walking fast with my head down. "No!" I shook my head. My mind was totally empty, all stirred up and empty, except for that one word, *"No!"*

I went over the lip of a ridge and doubled back along the top in case someone was chasing me. My legs ached. I collapsed into the grass at the base of a giant groundsel and gasped for breath. After a second I sat up and began watching the way I'd come to see if anyone would follow me.

Gradually my head started to clear. Mom had said Rick was her kid. . . . That meant that she had gotten pregnant before she got married. My mom had really done that. I shook my head.

Just then I saw movement along the top of the ridge. I lay flat against the base of the groundsel. The grass was wet and wiry against my face.

Uncle Paul came over the ridge about fifty yards from me. He stood still, looking, scanning the grass.

I froze. I was *not* ready to go back yet. Couldn't they leave me alone for a bit?

Lisa came over the ridge next to him. I could see her talking to him, but it was too windy to hear what they were saying. They split up and walked different directions along the top of the ridge. Lisa came towards me.

"Anika!" she called. "Aaanika!"

Part of me wanted to answer her, but if I did, I'd have

to face Mom and everything. I pressed myself lower in the grass. She got close enough I could hear her footsteps. Suddenly she stopped.

"Anika?" she said. I could hear her coming closer really fast. She'd seen me! What if she yelled for Uncle Paul?

I sat up and frantically shushed her, and motioned her to get down. She gave me a funny look, but she came over and got down beside me.

"What's wrong with you?" she whispered.

I just shook my head. It was too hard to say right out like that. I was glad Lisa had found me, if only she wouldn't tell.

It was like she was reading my mind because she said, "I'll have to tell them I found you. Running away doesn't work, remember?"

I nodded, remembering chasing after my cousin Tianna when she'd run away from boarding school.

We were both quiet for a second, then she said, "Dad's going to start looking for me in a minute."

"Look," I blurted. "I'm not really trying to run away. I just want time to think. Mom just told me that Rick is her kid."

There. I'd said it. It was out. Lisa's reaction didn't help. She stared at me with her mouth open, then squeaked, "Her *kid!*"

I nodded. What Lisa said next took me by surprise.

"Wow, that'll make people talk. I wonder if they'll still let her be a missionary with an illegitimate kid. Does your dad know?"

I hadn't been thinking of anybody but me. That was the first time I even thought about how Mom felt— about people talking about her. Suddenly the times I'd heard her crying came back to me, and what she'd said about worrying about Sandy and me. I felt hollow and sick. I didn't want Mom hurt. Suddenly I loved her so much. How could Rick do this to her?

"Yeah, Daddy knows," I said slowly.

"Then that's—uh-oh, there's Uncle Paul," Lisa said suddenly, interrupting herself.

I grabbed her. "Don't you dare tell!"

"He's going to find us in a minute anyway."

"Please? Really, I'm not running away."

She nodded. Then she put her hand on mine where I had hold of her arm. "It will be OK. God is strong enough for anything, remember? He got you to the top of the mountain, didn't he?"

My eyes stung like I was going to cry. Lisa got up and walked out from behind the groundsel.

After Lisa left I thought about her going back to the others. I realized I was very, very hungry and thirsty. All of a sudden I wanted to run after her, to go back with her. But if I went back everyone would look at me. It would be horrible. They would ask questions. Lisa was right; running away made things worse. I felt stupid—stupid and confused. I sat up and hugged my knees. The buckle on my fanny pack dug into my stomach. I fingered it absently, then my eyes opened wide.

I had food and water! Quickly I felt for my canteen, took it off my belt, and drank. Wow, that tasted good, but there were only about three swallows left. I took the last gulp and wiped off a drip that ran down my chin. There were still about six little boxes of raisins in my fanny pack. I fished one out.

Gradually a wild idea was taking shape in my head. I could go on down the mountain and find Daddy. That way I wouldn't have to face everybody by myself. Daddy would be with me. I could do it. We were planning to hike back to the lodge today, anyway. I'd just take a head start! I'd fill my canteen in the creek. I could talk to Daddy about everything. He'd understand.

I moved to the top of the ridge and lay so only my head stuck over. I could see the camp, and the creek, and the path. If I was careful to stay on the path, I could easily get down by myself. The trouble was there was no way I could get to the creek where it crossed the path without going almost into camp. I frowned. I'd just have to wait for water.

If I stayed on the back side of the ridge until I got to where the path came over, nobody could see me. I backed off the top of the ridge and started down.

It was easier to walk once I got to the path, but I didn't feel easy in myself. I fished another box of raisins out of my fanny pack and pried it open. Would Lisa tell? She didn't know that I'd started down. I could get in big trouble.

The sweet, sticky raisins made me thirstier. I pried the last raisins off the bottom of the box and walked faster, frowning. I had to somehow tell the others what I was doing without going back. I glanced at the raisin box in my hand. It was sticky, but it would be OK for writing a note on—if I had something to write with.

I kept going, looking uneasily over my shoulder. It would be *so* embarrassing if the others caught up now, especially having Rick look at me.

Way down, coming around a corner towards me, were three other people. That was it! I'd get them to tell the others what I was doing. That way, maybe Mom wouldn't be too mad.

It didn't take me long to get to the people. They were three big, blond men with walking sticks and big boots. They were walking one behind the other, in step.

"Hi!" I called, coming towards them. The front one nodded at me. They kept walking. I stopped to wait for them, figuring they'd stop when they got to me. They didn't even pause.

"Um, please, could you help me?" I asked, walking along beside them. Their faces looked tired. The first man seemed to be counting under his breath. He called out something, and all the men stopped exactly together like they were soldiers.

"Now," he said in a deep, heavily accented voice, "how can I help you?"

"Um, my mom and the people I came with are still at Teleki Valley camp. Could you tell them I'm OK, and I'm going down?" It sounded dumb, even to me.

"By yourself?" one of the other men asked.

I looked at him and gave a quick nod. "I have to."

"You have to?" he asked fiercely. Suddenly they all looked about eight feet tall. They were going to make me go with them!

I spun to run off.

"Girl!" the first man called. "How will we know who to tell?"

I stopped and looked back up at them and called, "Look for a man with a big red beard."

They nodded, and the second man asked, "How far to Teleki camp?"

"You're almost there," I called back.

"Danke!" he said, and they all waved. I looked up at

119

them, thinking that they were nice after all. The first man made a motion, the others got into step, and off they went. They looked like a huge six-legged insect all in step like that. I smiled and turned to go down.

I still felt scared about going down on my own. But it wasn't until it started raining that I realized I didn't even have my pack. I sucked in my breath. I'd forgotten all about it. How would Mom and them get an extra pack down?

"Well I'm not going back for it now!" I said to myself, scrambling around a puddle in the path.

I looked up at the sky, squinting against the fine rain. At least it wasn't raining really hard, and I had my jacket. I pulled the hood up over my head. *Even without the poncho, I'll be OK,* I thought, hoping that I was right.

I couldn't stop thinking about Rick. I'd always kind of wanted a brother, but not this way. He probably wasn't even a Christian. Mom had said it could wreck our family. What did she mean?

I stopped dead, jarring my sore heel, and squeaked right out loud, "Me? Acting like this?" I shook my head and licked the rainwater off my top lip. Could *I* wreck our family? I felt sick inside.

My hands were freezing from being wet. I dug my mittens out of my pockets.

"It's not my fault. It's Rick's!" I hissed through my teeth. "It is!"

Going down was harder than I thought it would be at first; way harder. I kept reminding myself that at least it was quicker going down than going up. My knees and thighs ached horribly from stopping myself to keep from going too fast. The blister on the back of my foot burned, and my toes hurt from hitting the end of my boots. I was sweating inside my jacket even though my face, hands, and legs were cold and wet.

I wanted to stop, just stop and rest. But I was afraid to have the others catch up because I couldn't keep going. Talk about humiliating! That fear was like a hand pushing me faster and faster.

Chapter
Ten

I clenched my teeth. I'd made it up the mountain. I could make it down! I was *not* going to wait and have the others catch up to me.

I stumbled and banged my sore heel on a rock.

"Ow!" I gasped, hopping on the other foot. A rock turned under my foot, and I fell down.

I sucked air through clenched teeth and held my sore foot. That's when I remembered that I *hadn't* made it up alone. Like those verses in Ephesians had said, God had helped me. I squirmed and got up, forcing myself not to limp. I didn't feel right about asking for God's help now. It was like my anger against Rick was in the way.

"Why did he have to show up, anyway?" I whispered furiously. "Why couldn't he just leave us alone?"

Now that I'd remembered those verses, it was like God was butting into my head. One part especially kept bugging me. The part that said, "I pray that your life will be strong in love and be built on love."

I shook my head furiously. I would not love Rick! He

was barging his way into *my* family. I pictured Mom walking with him, Sandy and Mom and Rick walking together. My eyes stung with tears.

I frowned and walked faster. I just had to find Daddy. He'd understand. In a hurry, I lunged over an extra-big clump of grass and fell hard. My sore heel hit a rock. Waves of pain shot up my leg. I gasped and grabbed my leg. Gradually the pain went down to a bearable level.

"This is crazy," I gasped and yanked on my boot. Wow! That hurt. I gritted my teeth and pulled harder. Gradually the boot slid off. I sat there letting the pain go down again, staring at my foot. My sock was bloody, right from my ankle to halfway down my foot. Gingerly I pulled the sock off, gritting my teeth when it stuck to my heel.

Gross! The whole back of my heel had no skin on it. Mom's bandage was all wadded up and stuck to my sock. There was absolutely no way I was going to put that boot back on. Even thinking about it made me cringe.

I looked around uneasily. There was no one in sight on the gray, rainy moorland. Already there were giant heather trees around.

I must be almost back down to the road, I thought. *Well, I'll just have to go barefoot.* I yanked off my other boot and sock, and started down again. My feet were tough—I mean, I went barefoot a lot. But this was different. Those gray rocks in the grass had sharp, jagged edges. The grass was wet, cold, and slippery.

The boots were hard to hang on to. I kept looking up the path to see if the others were catching up to me. Every time a blade of grass touched the back of my heel it stung like blazes.

Cold, gritty mud oozed between my toes. I stepped carefully around rocks and huge clumps of grass. My feet were freezing. It started raining harder. My jacket was like a heavy, wet, cold hand across my shoulders. I dropped one of my boots for about the tenth time.

I hurled the other boot down and stood there shivering. Nothing was going right! What if Daddy scolded me for running off? He probably would. He was always on Mom's side.

I glared at those stupid boots and blurted out, "I don't care what they say! I'm not carrying them any more."

I started down again, going as fast as I could. My jaw muscles ached from clenching my teeth to keep them from chattering. It started to pour. Even with my hood on, rain dripped off my bangs and into my eyes. I was so thirsty I kept licking the water off my lip.

"Hey, kid!" The voice sounded thin. It was coming from uphill. I spun to look, squinting through the rain.

Rick? Was that Rick? It was hard to tell for sure because he was still pretty far away, and it was raining so hard. I didn't wait to find out. I put my head down and ran.

Whack! I caught my foot on a tangle of tough grass and fell. Scrambling up, I skidded in the slick mud and fell again. My heel was still killing me.

"Kid! Take it easy!" He sounded closer. It *was* Rick!

I lunged to my feet and walked as fast as I could. He caught up and walked beside me. He loomed over me. I edged away. This couldn't be my brother!

"What's with you," he asked, "tearing off like that?"

"Where's *my* mom and them?" I asked over my shoulder, trying to walk away from him.

"I took off after you as soon as those Germans told us you were heading down. I don't think any of them know where I went. They were pitching things into packs so they could come after you. You made *your* mom really upset." He said *"your* mom" in a loud, ironic voice.

"*I* made her upset?" I yelled, stopping dead. "How about you? You barge in here from out of the blue and wreck everything! It's all *your* fault!"

He flinched like I'd hit him and glared at me out of bright blue eyes. Rain was dripping off his hood.

"Look, it's a pretty big shock for me too, actually seeing her . . . and you all. I wanted to find my birth mother, OK? Then I find out there are other kids. Besides that, you're so religious—missionaries, no less. Then you act like such a—" He swore. "Some religion! I just wanted to know . . ."

I ducked away from him, feeling very confused. The swearing had scared me. He seemed rough and angry, and he was so big. Still, when he talked about his birth mother (my mom?!), he seemed like a worried kid. What would it be like, wondering who your real mom was? Why couldn't things just be normal again?

"Leave me alone!" I blurted, shaking my wet bangs out of my eyes. I whirled and started walking away from him.

He stood there and let me go.

I started down the final slope onto the road, skidding in the mud and trying to protect my sore heel. I couldn't stop shivering. I could feel Rick looking at me and tried to walk straighter. My jacket seemed to weigh twice as much as my pack had.

A few seconds later he caught up to me again. "Kid, even if you hate me, I can't let you go on alone. Like, I've done quite a bit of backpacking. Staying soaked and cold like you are is real trouble. I've got to help you."

I kept going, but I walked slower. He'd said he'd help me even if I hated him. He was acting way more Christian than I was. I'd never felt this cold and miserable in my life before. I licked the drips from my bangs off my top lip and stopped walking. The rain had dropped to a light mist.

I stood there, half afraid, stiffly watching him out of the corner of my eye.

"Are you going to let me help you or not?" he demanded.

"I guess," I said.

I glanced up at him and caught him looking at me with an odd expression on his face. *This is my mother's child?* I wondered and ducked my head. My teeth were chattering, but I hardly noticed.

He shook his head and said, "Weird, isn't it, seeing each other for the first time."

"How," I asked between chatters, "how do you know you are my, I mean—"

He interrupted me, "Leave it!" he said, sounding almost angry. "Get off your wet stuff. I'll get you dry stuff from my pack."

I stared at him with my mouth open. Put on clothes from his pack? Here?

He turned away from me and started digging in his pack.

A violent shudder shook me. I ached all over. I swallowed hard. Being this cold was horrible. I'd have to do what he said.

"Come on, get the wet things off," he said roughly. "I won't turn around."

Taking a deep breath, I turned my back on him to unzip my jacket. My hands were so cold it was hard to hold on to the zipper. The jacket finally slid off my shoulders. I stood up straighter, glad to be rid of that soaking cold weight. The wind cut right through me. I tried to undo my jeans. The big rivet button at the top of the zipper wouldn't budge. My hands were too cold to get a good grip. I struggled madly, trying to get my hands to take hold. It would be horrible if I had to ask Rick to help me.

"Please, God," I whispered, trying desperately to get the button undone. Finally it came.

"Here, put these on," Rick said, holding out a pair of gray sweats behind his back.

As soon as I got them on, they felt dry and wonderful. I held them up with one hand and took the T-shirt he was holding out behind his back. It was impossible to hold up the baggy pants, hold on to a T-shirt, and get out of my sweatshirt at the same time, especially shivering as hard as I was. Finally I stuck the T-shirt between my knees, let the pants go, and struggled to yank off my sweatshirt. I wanted to do it really fast, but fast just wasn't one of the things my body would do right then.

Wow! The wind felt cold on my bare skin. I had the

T-shirt over my head when Rick said roughly, "You decent yet?"

"Almost," I stammered, then said, "OK," as I got the T-shirt all the way on.

He turned around and his mouth quirked up at the corner. I stood there clutching the huge baggy sweat pants with one hand. The T-shirt was down almost to my knees. *He didn't have to laugh!* I thought, then realized how stupid I must look and managed a shaky grin.

He gave me a smile and said, "You're a tough one, aren't you?"

I shook my head and said, "I'm still cold."

He nodded and started taking off his raincoat and jacket. "You'll have to put on my shirt and jacket."

I frowned and stammered between shivers, "How about you?"

"I'll be OK," he said, pulling his shirt off over his head.

He held out his shirt to me. When I pulled it on, the warmth came right through the T-shirt. I closed my eyes with relief.

"Um, you might want a belt to hold those pants up," Rick said, grinning. He pulled the belt out of my soaking jeans and held it out to me. We ended up staring at each other again. It seemed very unreal that this guy could be part of Mom.

He blinked, handed me the belt, and turned his back

on me to dig in his pack again. I remembered how he'd all of a sudden looked like Sandy just before I'd run off, but he didn't look like her now.

"How do you know you're Mom's kid?" I asked again.

He gave me a half angry look, then said, "I guess you have a right to know. See, Mom and Dad told me from when I was little that I was adopted, but when Mom died . . ." He paused.

Mom died! I thought, blinking with shock. It took me a second to realize he was talking about another mom. My head spun. He had another, totally different family of strangers.

". . . kind of complicated." I caught the end of a sentence. "I guess I can tell you while we wait for your mom and them to catch up."

The thought of waiting for everyone to catch up really snapped me out of it. "No!" I blurted. "I'm still going down. I want to talk to Daddy first."

He jerked his head away from me, and looked into the distance. After an uneasy pause he said, "Yeah, there's still your righteous missionary father. Um, maybe you can tell me. Does he know about me?"

"Didn't Mom tell you when you talked to her?" I asked.

He smiled. "Mostly she made me talk about myself. I didn't get a chance to ask many questions." For a second he stood there with this half smile on his face. He shook himself and said, "I can't believe I've actually talked to my birth mom. For a religious nut, she wasn't too bad."

"She's not a nut!" I blurted. My stomach felt odd. It was strange to hear him talking about Mom like she was someone totally different than the person I knew.

"Do you know?" he asked.

"What?" I asked, trying to remember what we were talking about.

"If your father knows."

"Oh," I said, and I swallowed, remembering the conversations I'd heard in the night. They made sense now. "Yeah, he knows that you're alive, that Mom had another kid. He said they'd been praying for you for fifteen years, ever since they got to be Christians."

"He told you that?" Rick asked, sounding surprised.

"Well, not exactly," I said. "I heard them talking the night after—" I stopped and whirled on him. "You wrote to her! The letter was from you!"

"No, but the people that were helping me look did. Why?"

"Nothing," I said. It didn't matter now. Suddenly I wanted desperately to talk to Daddy. He wasn't different. He was still just my normal father. I wanted to be with him, to hold on to someone that hadn't changed.

"Thanks for helping me and everything, but I'm going down now. I've got to see Daddy."

"Does he know I'm here?" Rick asked, moving in front of me and stopping.

"How am I supposed to know?" I said, trying to push past him. "Did it say in the letter?"

"No . . . no, it didn't. I just came when I found out where she was. I mean I had the money, and— Look," he said, interrupting himself, "how are you going to find your father?"

"He's supposed to come up the forest road as far as he can to meet us with the car. I want to get there first."

He frowned, thinking, then said, "You're dry now, but you're barefoot. You sure you can do it?"

I nodded. "My feet are tough. It will be OK now that we're on the road."

He bit his lower lip, still frowning. He seemed so big, blocking my way. Everything was so weird. This big person standing close to me, my brother? I felt detached, like I was watching this happen to some other kid. When Rick spoke, I jumped.

"OK, I'll go back up and tell your mom you are OK . . . Um, you'll tell your dad I'm here, kind of break it to him before he sees me . . . ?"

Rick looked worried when he said that. It struck me all over again how he was like a kid still, like me. Suddenly I wasn't mad about him any more.

Still, I didn't answer his question at first. Even if I

wasn't mad, did I want to help him get into our family? Mom and Daddy would let him in anyway. They were like that. *That verse about being "strong in love" fits them,* I thought, frowning.

Suddenly I was glad about that, really glad that our family was strong in love. I wanted to be part of it. Just as I opened my mouth to say I'd help, Rick said, "Never mind," in a rough voice and took off hiking up the road.

"Rick!" I called. It came out in a kind of squeak. I swallowed and tried again. *"Rick!"* He didn't even turn his head.

I stared after him, feeling sad. "He must really think I'm a jerk," I whispered. At least I could go tell Daddy for him like he asked. I sighed and headed downhill.

Chapter
Eleven

Slick mud oozed between my toes. Sometimes sharp rocks under the mud scraped across my feet when I slipped.

"I'm sorry for being such a pain, Jesus," I whispered as I trotted and slithered down the road, trying to ignore my sore heel. "Also please help me with this whole thing. Help me be strong in love," I sighed. It wasn't going to be easy, but then the mountain hadn't been easy either and God helped me with that.

"Also please help Rick see that I'm not as much of a jerk as he thinks. Don't let him think that Christians are horrible because of me," I whispered.

Every time I came around a corner I kept hoping and looking for our car. That got me thinking about Daddy. How would he feel to have Rick here?

Suddenly I sucked in my breath and stopped. Did Rick have a different father somewhere? Daddy hadn't talked like Rick was his kid. I stood there biting my lip.

"Of course, stupid. Daddy isn't his father," I muttered

and started walking again. I wondered who was. Some guy in Mom's high school class? Thinking about it made my world feel loose from its foundations. Trying to think of Mom as a mixed-up teenager like . . . like . . . maybe like Jordie Penner, that tenth-grade girl who'd gotten pregnant. Nothing was the same as I thought before.

Mist settled between the dripping, mossy trees. The rolled-up cuffs on Rick's sweats were soaked and muddy. They slapped my feet and the ground with every step. The steady *swack, swack, swack* sounded loud in the quiet forest as I slogged downhill.

At least animals will hear me coming, I thought, then went back to puzzling about Mom. I wondered when she had told Daddy about having a kid before and how he had felt. Everything seemed double.

Mom was someone totally different to Rick than she was to me. Also if that man who was Rick's father thought of her, he thought of a mixed-up teenager. It seemed like everyone was covered by layers and layers of pictures. Each picture was another person's idea of who they were. Nobody really knew anyone else at all.

I frowned. All I knew about people was my picture of them, and I'd just found out that my picture of Mom was . . . was . . . well, *wasn't* . . . wasn't *what?* I bit my lip. I'd thought of her more as just my mother. She was a whole different person besides. Who else was Daddy? I slowed down.

A crashing noise and a hoarse *whoop* brought me skidding to a halt. I jerked my head up in time to see a troupe of colobus monkeys leaping off through the tree-tops. Their long black-and-white hair flew behind them like cloaks. Gradually my heart stopped pounding. It was just monkeys. That's when I remembered Mom's story about the lady and the buffalo. There *could* be buffalo and elephant on the road!

Suddenly my throat felt dry and tight. I swallowed hard. Why hadn't I stayed with Rick? I looked back up the road, but it was empty and quiet under the misty trees. Just for a second, through the gap in the treetops over the road, I saw the peaks of the mountain, black and jagged through the cloud. That psalm Daddy had read flashed into my head.

"I look up to the hills. But where does my help come from? My help comes from the Lord. He made heaven and earth."

I couldn't remember the rest except that it was about God keeping us safe and never sleeping.

"Thanks, God," I whispered. "Please help me to get down to Daddy OK." I squirmed, and added, "Whoever he is."

How was I ever going to get things balanced again?

I started down again, but I was still scared. What if the noise my pants were making wasn't loud enough? Taking a deep breath, I started singing. I mean, I didn't have a great voice, but at least the animals would know I was coming and hopefully get out of the way.

My voice sounded too loud echoing back off the trees. I wanted to stop, to be quiet, to hide. For a second I did stop, but it was no good standing there being afraid. I took a deep breath and kept singing even louder.

The rhythmic slapping noise of my soaked and muddy pant cuffs kept time. I'd been singing anything that came into my head, including little-kid songs like "Jesus Loves Me."

I sang it again. "Jesus loves me, this I know, for the Bible tells me so," I sang, and I paused. *He does!* I thought. *And he knows who I am, too. Not who anybody thinks I am, but who I really am.* I frowned, figuring it out. Jesus knows who people really are—not like the pictures we have of each other, but the real person.

I sang it over again twice more, thinking about it. Halfway through the third time two people came around a corner in the road walking uphill. I shut up in a hurry and felt my face get hot. Moving way over to the side of the road, I went by them with my head down.

Just after they'd passed me I realized they might have

seen Daddy on the way up. They'd know how far downhill Daddy was.

"Hey!" I yelled, spinning to look back at them. They stopped and looked at me. "Um, excuse me," I stammered, realizing I hadn't been very polite. "Did you see a gray car? I mean was there one by the road with a man waiting?"

"Yeah, we did," one of them answered in American English. "It's about a quarter of a mile back. By the way, good singing, kid." They both laughed.

Without even saying thank you, I took off. Only a quarter of a mile! I even forgot to sing. One of the pant cuffs came unrolled and tripped me flat onto my face in the mud. I jumped up and jerked it out of the way impatiently.

"Anika? Anika! It *is* you."

I whirled. Daddy was there, walking up the road towards me. I yelled and ran to him.

He held me off with both hands on my shoulders. "Easy, easy, you're covered in mud."

I grinned at him. He was my very own dad. Look at the way he was holding on to me so I wouldn't get him muddy. He hated us messing him up.

"You're my dad!" I said, shakily. "You might be other people too, but you're still my dad."

He gave me a very weird look, then he did a double take and looked me up and down from head to foot.

"What on earth happened to you? Those aren't your clothes!" His hands tightened convulsively on my shoulders. "What happened? Is Mom OK?" He shook me. "Where are the others?"

"They're OK," I gasped. Suddenly everything overwhelmed me and I felt like crying. I hate crying. I spun away from him and furiously rubbed at my eyes with a muddy fist.

"You sure they're OK?" Daddy asked again.

I nodded without turning.

Daddy gently turned me back around. "Let's get back to the car, then tell me how you got separated from your mother and where these clothes came from."

I followed him, trying to get back into control.

He got an old towel out of the trunk and covered up the car seat before he'd let me sit down. That made me feel better in an odd sort of way. It was such a normal thing for him to do.

"Well?" he asked, half smiling, "what did you get yourself into this time?"

"It's Rick," I blurted. "See, these are his clothes and I ran from Mom. I mean not really on purpose, but— Anyway, I made it to the top, only me and Uncle Paul did, but—"

"Stop!" Daddy said, holding up his hand and laughing. "How about if I ask questions and you answer."

"But, Daddy," I interrupted. "Don't you get it? *Rick* is here, Mom's other kid."

He'd been looking up the road, but when I said that, he jerked around to face me. "How do you know about that?" he demanded.

"Daddeeee, he's here! He's that guy that kept staring at us at the lodge, remember? These are his clothes," I said, pointing at myself. "See, I was really mad at first. I didn't want it to be true. . . ."

Daddy wasn't listening to me. He was staring into space past my shoulder. Suddenly he interrupted, "Your mother's talked to him?"

I nodded and didn't say anything. His eyes were too fierce.

"You made a big scene, ran off, and made things harder for her?"

It wasn't like he was actually asking me, or even paying attention to me. My mouth was too dry to say anything. He stared past me for a couple of seconds, frowning hard, and then said, "I'm going to walk on up to meet her. Rick has to deal with me as well if he wants to have anything to do with my family."

He looked at me like he was seeing me again, and his eyes got kinder. "You'll be OK here. We'll talk properly later."

I looked after him anxiously as he started up the

road. Maybe Rick was right to be worried about him. I sighed. Nothing was turning out right. Daddy hadn't even heard me say I'd made it to the top.

The gritty, cold, muddy cuffs of the pants I had on were really bugging me. The huge T-shirt I had on covered me down to the knees, so I pulled the pants off.

That made me feel a bit better, on the outside anyway. *How far were the others behind me, anyway?* I wondered, peering up the empty road. There was more fog now so I couldn't see as far. I poked around the car looking for something to drink. Finally I found a Thermos under the back seat. It had milky tea in it from the trip to the mountain. I took a huge gulp. Cool and sweet, it filled my dry mouth and throat.

It seemed like everybody was mad at me now. I swallowed hard, blinking back the tears. More than anything I wanted our family to be OK. I wanted us to be strong in love, God's love. The thing was, nobody even knew that. They all thought I was still against Rick.

Suddenly I wanted to read those verses over again. When I was poking around I'd seen a Bible in the glove compartment. I sniffed hard, then fished it out and looked up Ephesians, trying not to get too much mud on the pages.

It said, "I ask the Father in his great glory to give you the power to be strong in spirit. He will give you that strength through his Spirit. I pray that Christ will live in your hearts because of your faith. I pray that your life will be strong in love and be built on love." It kept talking about how big Christ's love is and how he wants us to understand it.

"Then you can be filled with the fullness of God," it said. "With God's power working in us, God can do much, much more than anything we can ask or think of."

I took a big breath of relief and put the Bible back. It made so much sense now. "Please make me so I can do the right thing and not be scared," I prayed. "I can't by myself. I just keep blowing it."

I hugged my knees, feeling better. *Even if everything, and everybody, was different than I thought before, God is steady,* I thought, then sighed. I was so tired that I felt numb. My head fell back, and I was asleep.

The sound of the car door opening half woke me, then Mom's voice was in my ears.

"Anika? Anika? You're OK!" Mom's arms came around me in a warm hug.

"I'm sorry, Mom," I mumbled, trying to make my mouth work. "Please don't be mad. I'm sorry."

"I'm just glad you're OK," she said and gave me a tight squeeze.

I heard other voices and struggled to sit up. Mom let go of me, and somebody laughed. That's when I realized what I must look like. I jerked the T-shirt down to cover my legs.

"Why did you run away?" Sandy demanded.

I didn't answer.

"Leave it," Daddy said. "We'll talk later. Let's get back and get you all cleaned up and fed."

"I say amen to that," boomed Uncle Joey.

Going down, the car was even more crowded than it had been coming up because Rick got in too. Lisa and I ended up squashed in the back seat with Rick and the packs. The four grown-ups and Sandy and Traci squeezed into the front.

I kept getting bumped up against Rick. I wanted to explain that I was sorry, that I wanted to help him now, but I couldn't with everyone listening. I wondered if Uncle Joey and Uncle Paul even knew who Rick was. Nobody talked. The air was thick with things nobody would ask.

Back at the lodge, Lisa and I went straight to the showers. That hot shower poured over me, washing off the cold muddy ache of the last two days.

"Hey, Anika, hurry up!" Lisa yelled at me. "I want a turn too."

"OK already," I answered, turning to let the hot water pour over my back. I closed my eyes in bliss.

"Anika!" Lisa yelled. I didn't answer. A second later I

yelled and nearly jumped out of my skin. A big wave of freezing cold water splashed down over me.

"Liiisaa!" I yelled. "You didn't have to throw cold water on me, you turkey!"

She stopped laughing long enough to say, "So get out then. You've been in there for ages."

I wrapped a towel around myself and got out, sticking my tongue out at her.

It felt good to laugh with her, but I sobered quickly when she said, "I think you're lucky finding a big brother. All I've got is Alex. Ugh!"

She kept talking about how cute Rick was, and how she wished he was her brother. I squirmed. I didn't want to talk about it—at least not until things got sorted out.

"Anika!" Mom was calling from the door.

"Just a sec," I answered, stuffing my legs into clean jeans.

Sandy was with her. Both of them were already clean. "Listen," she said, "Daddy and I are going to spend some time with Rick this evening. I want you both to eat supper with Uncle Joey and Uncle Paul."

"Mommm!" Sandy said, "he's our brother!"

"I know," Mom said. "I hope you'll get a chance to spend time with him. But for now, Daddy and I need to talk to him."

"Mommm . . . ," Sandy protested again.

I didn't say anything. I felt too confused inside.

"Look, girls, what you can do is pray. I need your prayers and so do Rick and Dad. I've got to go, they're waiting. I love you both, and no matter what happens you're my very own girls."

Mom hugged Sandy, then me. Just as she was letting go, I whispered, "Mom, I really need to talk to him."

She just patted my shoulder and left. I think she was trying not to cry.

At the table everybody talked about the mountain. I kept looking around for Mom, Dad, and Rick. When I looked at Sandy she seemed small and worried. I wanted to switch places and sit by her, but I was too numb to move. Being warm, full, and clean made me so drowsy it seemed like a thick layer of sleepiness was gumming up my thoughts like Vaseline.

Right after supper, Uncle Paul told us to go to bed. "Your folks and Rick are in God's hands," he said.

When he left, Sandy and I were finally alone. She'd looked so worried at supper. I wanted to explain about how God was steady no matter what, to make her feel better. As we got ready for bed, I tried to think how to tell her.

"Sandy?" I said, "Um, see . . . I found these verses that say that—"

She whirled on me. "Don't talk to me about how I should be good! You're the one that ran off and made the whole day horrible!"

I stared at her with my mouth open. I never thought Sandy would be mad at me too.

"It's all your fault!" she yelled and started to cry.

"It is not!" I answered then swallowed hard. Sandy and me fighting wouldn't help. Besides, she was partly right. I sighed and said, "Um, sorry for doing that. I already told Mom sorry."

Her head was down, and seeing the little soft swirls of hair at the top of her neck made me feel like protecting her. "Look, I didn't make Rick come. I didn't make Mom have a kid without being married when she was a teenager."

Sandy twisted away from me and sobbed harder.

"Um," I said, uneasily reaching out my hand and pulling it back again. "See, I was really scared that everything was wrecked. That's why I wouldn't let it be true. But now I want to be strong in love like Mom and Daddy maybe are. If we stick together with God, you and me will be OK, even if stuff turns out wrong." *I hope,* I added in my head to myself.

Suddenly Sandy whirled and hugged me around the chest. I staggered, then caught my balance and hugged her back. We stood there like that for a long time.

Finally I let go and said, "We'd better go to bed like they said."

She nodded, and her hair tickled my nose. She let go without looking up and jumped into bed. I climbed into bed and stretched out my aching body.

"Anika?" Sandy's voice sounded small in the dark. "Anika? Can we pray?"

"Um-hum," I said, already half asleep.

"Dear Jesus," she said, "please let our family be OK, and let Rick get to know you too like Mom wants. Let them . . ."

I went to sleep right in the middle of her prayer.

"Anika, wake up." It was Daddy's voice. I ungummed my eyes. It was bright daylight out. Birds were singing. Rubbing my eyes, I sat up.

"Come on, we've got to get packed up to go. We decided to let you sleep, but it's almost noon now, and everything else is loaded up."

"Where's Rick?" I blurted. "Is everything OK?"

Daddy laughed and knuckled my head. "Yes, we're OK. Rick is just leaving to take his rental car back. . . ."

I never heard the rest of the sentence because I jumped out of bed, grabbed my jeans and a T-shirt, and pushed past Daddy to the bathroom.

"I have to catch him," I whispered, hopping on one

foot jerking my jeans on. "He can't leave thinking I don't care."

I yanked my T-shirt over my head, tore out the door, and ran for the parking lot. He was still there, just getting into a fancy sports car.

"Rick!" I yelled. "Rick, please wait!"

He checked and then kept moving.

"Rick, please listen this time," I panted, running up to him.

He stood up slowly and looked at me.

"Um . . . ," I said, trying to catch my breath and collect my thoughts. It wasn't so easy to know what to say now that he was looking at me. "Um, I just wanted to say sorry for being such a jerk."

He just kept looking at me, so I went on, "I was scared, see. I thought everything was getting wrecked, but now I want to be strong in love. In God's love. Even if Mom isn't who I thought, God's the same. . . ." He was looking at me so odd that I just kind of stopped talking.

After a second I said, "Well, sorry for being so awful to you," and turned to go.

"Hey," he called after I'd gone a few steps.

I turned. "You're OK," he said, grinning, and added, "even if you are a little weird." He shook his head and muttered, "All this 'God' stuff. Talk about religious!"

I stood on one foot, not sure how to respond. Then he grinned again and thumped my shoulder and said, "I got to go, kid. See you at Amboseli Game Park."

I watched him drive off, wondering what he meant about Amboseli. Maybe Mom and Dad invited him to come there with us. Having a new brother that didn't know God and getting used to my mom being different than I thought wasn't going to be easy, but then God never promised easy.

Strong in God's love, strong enough for any mountain, I thought as I walked slowly back toward the lodge, smiling.

If you've enjoyed the **Anika Scott** books,
you'll want to read these additional series
from Tyndale House!

Elizabeth Gail
Join this delightful heroine in 21 exciting
adventures, including these recent releases!

#20 The Mystery of the Hidden Key
*Libby's discovery of a lost key eventually
leads her to help two runaway boys.*

#21 The Secret of the Gold Charm
*Libby's good luck charm backfires when she discovers
it is a stolen piece from the school museum.*

Cassie Perkins

#1 No More Broken Promises

#2 A Forever Friend

#3 A Basket of Roses

#4 A Dream to Cherish

#5 The Much-Adored Sandy Shore

#6 Love Burning Bright

#7 Star Light, Star Bright

#8 The Chance of a Lifetime

#9 The Glory of Love

You can find Tyndale books at fine bookstores everywhere.
If you are unable to find these titles at your local bookstore,
you may write for ordering information to:

**Tyndale House Publishers
Tyndale Family Products Dept.
Box 448
Wheaton, IL 60189**